Unbridled

Enjoy!

Susan Fawer

10/2018

ALSO BY SUSAN LOWER

SILVER WIND TRILOGY
Forgotten Reins—Book One
Unbridled—Book Two
Silver Stirrups—Book Three (coming soon)

THE BRIDES OF ANNIE CREEK NOVELLA SERIES
The Fruitcake Bride
The Thimble Bride (coming soon)

SHORT STORIES
"Emma's Dilemma"

PLANET MITCH SERIES FOR KIDS AGES 7–12
The Lost Star—Book One
The Black Eyed Galaxy—Book Two
(Available June 2016)
Out of This World—Book Three
(Available September 2016)
Attack of the Knit Knox—Book Four
(Available December 2016)

Unbridled

Silver Wind Trilogy—Book Two

SUSAN LOWER

Time Glider
Books

Published in Williamsport, Pennsylvania by Time Glider Books. Time Glider Books is a trademark of Time Glider Books, LLC.

Time Glider Books, LLC, books may be purchased in bulk for educational, business, fund-raising, or sales promotional use. For information, please email bulkorders@timegliderbooks.com

ISBN: 1945274905
ISBN-13: 978-1-945274-90-9

4 5 6 7 8 9 10 11 12   23 22 21 20 19 18 17 16

A person may think their own ways are right,
but the LORD weighs the heart.
Proverbs 21:2 (NIV)

.

CHAPTER 1

"Come on Jen, don't be that way."

Jenny Anderson stared at the man who'd taken her out to dinner, sat beside her in church every Sunday this year, and just confessed he was a family man.

Only his wife and children lived in Indiana.

For a moment, she didn't think she'd heard him right. Nevertheless, by the look of his face, he was dead serious. She took a deep breath, her heart rattling in her chest.

All the while he'd been here working for the construction company in Shelbyville, Kentucky, he'd been courting her. He'd invited her to dinner just three days after his company started construction on the equine clinic where she worked.

Her cheeks turned cold as the blood drained from her face. Unable to speak, she turned on her heel and strode out of the clinic. In the parking lot, she reached for the door handle of a red diesel truck.

"Didn't you hear what I said?" He followed her.

Oh, she'd him heard all right. In fact, she was certain everyone inside the clinic had stopped to stretch an ear toward their conversation.

He grabbed her by the arm.

Jenny's gaze fell to his hand. How many times had she held that hand so lovingly, just this past week? She looked up at him, holding her breath as if it would hold back the dam of tears building behind her eyes.

"If you don't mind," it took every ounce of her will power to hold steady. "I have a rescue that needs picked up."

"Then I'll go with you."

Jenny shook her head, biting her lip against any further words.

"So this is how it's going to be?"

This was the way it *had* to be. Opening the truck door and climbing inside the driver's seat, she pried a set of keys from her jean pocket. Avoiding taking one last look at the man who shattered her dreams of becoming his wife, she placed the key in the ignition. Why else would he have come at noon bearing gifts and wearing his best clothes?

"You're nothing but a bible thumper," he yelled.

She turned the key and the roar of the truck's engine drowned out whatever words he said next. It was probably better this way.

She glanced in the rear-view mirror, relieved that at least the trailer was hitched. As she steered the truck out of the clinic's parking lot, her chest became heavy, and each breath more difficult.

She watched from her side-view mirror as he tossed down his hat and balled his fist as she drove away.

Jenny inhaled deeply through her nose and exhaled through her mouth, but it was no use.

She pulled out onto the main road. Her heart torn by one man's misleading love and her love and fear for Christ.

"Thou shall not commit adultery," she whispered. Was she guilty of such a sin even now? She prayed a silent prayer of forgiveness.

How could he? Her knuckles turned white as she gripped the steering wheel. *All these months*! They'd even sat in church together!

A lump formed in her throat. She turned left at the crossroads, following the signs toward the highway.

Her nose stung. She tried to concentrate on the rescue that she needed to pick up. Since she, her twin brother Josh, and her best friend Sarah started Silver Wind Equine Rescue over a year ago, they'd received regular calls to pick up surrendered horses.

Right now, however, Jenny felt she was the one needing rescued.

It wasn't fair! Why couldn't she be happy like Sarah was with Michael? Hadn't God brought them back together after they'd been separated for all these years?

Good things come to those who wait, she smirked. She wasn't a teenager anymore. No, it was her friend Sarah, who'd gotten herself in trouble during their teenage years. Jenny had spent her time ministering through the Worth Waiting For program.

Now who would wait for her? Most all of the nice guys at church were either married or older and still living with their mothers.

She choked back a sob.

She'd been so certain when he approached her at the clinic, that Brad had finally come to propose. *Oh Lord, why did you let this go on for so long?*

As she merged onto the highway, an eighteen-wheeler whizzed past. She braced the steering wheel feeling the trailer sway behind her. The truck became a blur of black going down the highway, or perhaps it was her vision that grew blurry as her cheeks became damp. She swiped at the tears rolling down her cheeks.

Suddenly, the truck gained a burst of energy. Jenny frowned. From her side view mirror, she spotted the sun glinting off the aluminum trailer.

Her heart sank into her stomach. She watched as the trailer crossed two lanes, clipped the back wheel of a motorcycle, and veered into the grassy dike between the opposing highways.

Immediately, she slammed on the brakes.

CHAPTER 2

Cade Sheridan's whole life seemed to go in slow motion. His motorcycle tilted into a sixty mile-per-hour slide down the outer lane of the highway. It was like riding the spinner at the carnival when he was young. So fast, yet everything became slow and made him dizzy. He rode the shiny side of his motorcycle with the sound of metal against pavement roaring in his ears.

He leapt from his motorcycle and scrambled off the highway, rolling and crawling on his belly. An instant later, metal met metal as an eighteen-wheeler ran over his motorcycle like it was yesterday's road kill.

He heard the high piercing squall of the eighteen-wheeler hit its brakes and come to a screaming halt.

Cade sat up at the edge of the highway. He patted his chest and his arms. His leather jacket was torn. Yet, to his relief, his arms were still in the sleeves.

Unsteadily, he got to his feet.

Several cars slowed and pulled over. A red truck pulled up behind him.

He gazed out at the metal massacre. His motorcycle lay scattered in a dozen bits across the highway. He reached up and tried to unbuckle his helmet. His fingers fumbled with the metal buckle.

"You alright?" the owner of the eighteen-wheeler jumped out of his truck and ran towards him. "I've called it in, help is on the way."

He couldn't get the visor on his helmet to lift. Its cracked hinge prevented it from moving upwards. He stared across at the shattered pieces of his motorcycle and stumbled back.

"Here, let me help you."

Cade turned. A red haired woman stood before him with tears streaking down her face. She appeared out of nowhere, like a mirage under the hot sun. Was he in shock? He became weak in the knees. He needed to sit down before he crumbled to the side of the road.

"Help is on the way," he heard the truck driver yell again.

"I'm so sorry," she cried. "Are you okay?"

He shook his head, unsure if the rattle he heard came from his motorcycle or a piece of his brain. Slowly, he looked at her.

Her green eyes glistened in their watery state. Mesmerized by those eyes, he kept his focus on her as he reached again for the strap of his helmet. She brushed his fingers away and tugged on the straps.

Sirens sounded in the distance.

"Don't go to sleep on me now, stay awake," she said.

He'd closed his eyes at the sheer relief of her loosening his chinstrap. He tried, but opening his eyes even to squint at her became a struggle.

The pavement had been hard. His motorcycle had been hard. His life had been hard. But now, he felt everything lifting away from him, except for those eyes.

He felt a final tug on the strap, and it fell away from his chin.

"Better not take that off till the paramedics get here," someone said.

"I'm so sorry," she said.

Sorry for what?.

Then his world went black.

CHAPTER 3

In the hospital, Cade lay in a narrow bed with a thin sheet covering his bare legs and an even thinner blanket lying over his aching ribs. He groaned. His head pounded and the gritty taste of dirt lingered in his mouth.

His stomach grumbled. At least that part of him still functioned fine. His entire body ached down to his toes.

Outside the doorway, he spotted a nurse and called out. His voice came out rough sounding as if he'd spent the night gurgling rocks. No wonder his mouth tasted so foul.

"Good morning."

He turned his head and squinted against the bright sunlight streaming through the window. A woman stood from the chair beside his bed.

"Crystal?" He blinked, blinked until the vision of his ex-wife faded.

This woman had dark red hair and her green eyes were wide with alarm.

Reality slowly seeped in, and he winced.

How long had he been like this?

"I'm Jenny Anderson. We kind of met at the accident." Her brows furrowed and she asked, "A-are you okay? Can I get you s-something?"

"Yeah, something to drink and a couple of aspirin would be nice." Wasn't it just a few hours ago, that he'd been cruising down highway sixty-four on his motorcycle? What kind of fool would take a trailer out on the highway without first making sure it was hitched? He'd been lucky. Had the trailer crossed in front of him, he, too, may have ended up like his motorcycle.

She took a little black book from her hands and laid it on the edge of his bed. She got a cup from the bedside stand and poured him some water from the pitcher. He pulled himself up a little taller in his pillow and grabbed for the bed controller. She held out a cup as he adjusted the bed so he could sit up.

He took a few sips of water. It stung his throat and he winced to swallow. His ribs pinched as he breathed, and he knew at least one of them was broken.

"I-I'll see if I-I can find a nurse." She darted from around him and headed out into the hallway.

"Yeah," he muttered, "You do that."

He retrieved the black book she laid beside him, flipped through the pages, and then tossed the book over on the vacant chair by his bed.

She appeared again in the doorway. "A nurse is on the way," she said.

A male nurse whose name tag said 'Jim' slipped past her and brought him a small paper cup with pills. "So, I see you're awake."

"You say that as if it's a good thing." He took the pills all at once and accepted another cup of water. He swallowed, drained the cup, and looked back at Jenny.

"That was some tumble. I think I'd sleep a couple of days, too, if something like that happened to me."

"You were there." He remembered the eyes. Sad. Vibrant. They lingered with him in his dreams.

"Nope, can't say I was." Jim picked up Cade's wrist to check his pulse.

Her eyes fell to Jim's watch as he counted the seconds. Cade ignored the male nurse. His gaze remained locked on Jenny's face. She was the one. The one who caused all of this.

"How are you feeling?" Jim asked.

"Like I've been hit by a Mack truck," Cade said.

Jim laughed. "I'd say you're feeling just about right then."

Her face turned ghostly white beneath those short choppy dark red tresses. She appeared like a pixie from inside a fairytale. Although, he knew this was no fairytale. This was real. As real as her glossy pink lips.

When Jim finished checking vitals, he glanced between the two of them. "Doc will be in shortly to say 'Howdy'."

Cade watched as Jim made a note on his chart at the door and disappeared down the hall.

While his mind recollected the accident, his eyes strayed down to a pair of red cowboy boots.

He released a sigh, irate with himself for having noticed.

"I'm sorry about what happened to you."

A chill ran up his arms. So this is why she'd come—apologize. He gave her another long look, noting her wariness. *Well, at least one of us feels better now.*

"Are you cold? I can get you another blanket."

He cleared his throat. "I take it you're responsible for me being here?"

She chewed on the inside of the bottom of her lip and clasped her hands together in front of her.

"You're the owner of the trailer that nearly killed me, aren't you?"

"Well ... sort of." She took a few steps toward his bed.

"Sort of?" He wanted to rip her up one side and tear her down the other, but something about her vivid green eyes, and pale cheeks held his outburst at bay. That and he figured it wouldn't do any good. What was done was done, and like everything else in his life, there was no going back. Besides, she had guilt written across that pretty little forehead of hers and appeared distressed enough for both of them.

Shorter and shapelier than his Crystal, she reminded him of what he once lost. Motorcycles were replaceable. Mercy have it, he was still alive. His past was no longer salvageable.

"The truck and the trailer belong to the equine rescue I work for. I didn't know it wasn't hitched. You see, I just broke up with my boyfriend and I was upset, so I ...." Her voice trailed off.

He gawked at her for a long moment.

"I-I guess I am the last person you expected to see," she finished saying.

"You got that right."

"I contacted the insurance company, and I've assured the driver of the eighteen-wheeler that it wasn't all his fault." She gulped. "The insurance will cover your motorcycle, but it's going to take a few days to assess the liabilities and get it all settled. In the meantime, is there anyone I can contact? Family? Friends? All they found in your wallet was a few pictures, some cash, and your driver's license."

"That's what I usually keep in there," Cade said.

She brushed back a wisp of hair that had slipped down over her eye. "I just wanted to make sure you were okay. Nobody should ever be left in a hospital alone. Are you sure I can't call someone for you?"

If it hadn't been for the sudden shot of pain in his ribs, he might have given her a third glance. Instead, he turned his head and winced. "Don't bother."

She came closer, touching him on the shoulder. "Please, let me help you. It's the least I can do."

He laughed to fight the next surge of pain.

She lifted her chin a notch and forced a smile that didn't come near to reaching her eyes. "Well ..." She expelled a long breath. "If there isn't anything I can do for you then ..." She was silent for a long moment.

She could have made sure she checked the hitch on that trailer before hitting the highway, but as he reminded himself, there was no going back now. His mind felt foggy, probably from the pain medications the nurse gave him starting to kick it. He would need his phone, a new motorbike, and he was going to have to figure out what day this was, but his pride kept him from asking. So he gave her a hard stare, like he did every new horse he assessed before training it. There was a lot you could learn about a horse, or even a person when you held them under a stare.

She tilted her chin down and met his stare square on. There was a spark in those eyes of a challenge. Neither one of them spoke for a long minute. He got the feeling that inside, she was one stubborn filly.

Someone wearing squeaky shoes went down the hall and broke the trance between them.

She tore her gaze from his. Glancing toward the door, then back at him, she said, "I'd really like to call someone for you. Make sure you're okay."

He gave a curt nod, knowing that he should have been more appreciative of her concern. If there had been any person he could call, he might have taken her up on the offer.

"Thanks, but as you can see I'm capable of making a call."

Jenny pushed back that same strand of hair that had slipped over her eye again. She ducked her head, walked around his bed, and picked up a small leather handbag.

He watched as she turned to leave. "Don't forget to take that with you." He pointed to the black book.

Hesitantly, she took the Bible. As she left, he chided himself for noting the way her body swayed with grace upon her exit.

CHAPTER 4

All afternoon Jenny couldn't stop thinking of Cade Sheridan. Knowing it was the right thing to do, she had gone to the hospital every morning since the accident. According to the nurses, Jenny was the only one who came to visit him or called to check on him.

Now that he was awake, there was no reason for her to return. That was what she told herself. Reminding herself over and over again he didn't need her help. He had said as much before she left this morning.

Yet, she couldn't let go of this feeling that Cade Sheridan needed her help.

Of course, none of what happened was her fault. How was she supposed to know the truck had been parked with the hitch and ball resting atop each other without being locked together?

After supper Sarah invited her out on the porch to swing. She and Sarah had been best friends since the summer they all met at Kingsley's Estate. Jenny's twin brother, Josh, included.

Jenny had watched Sarah struggle through the loss of both her parents, teenage motherhood, and fulfilling her dream.

A dream, Jenny and Josh both shared with Sarah.

Now as Jenny gazed out at the barn filled with horses and the pastures lined with strands of wire fencing glinting in the harsh rays of the retiring sun, Jenny couldn't believe how far they had come.

How long would it have taken Sarah to tell Michael he was the father of Sarah's son if Jenny had not slipped Michael that letter?

Yet, now the one thing stuck on Jenny's mind was Cade Sheridan.

This was Brad's doing. If he hadn't made her so upset, then she wouldn't have taken off like she did.

All she wanted that day was to get away from Brad.

As she settled down into the porch swing, she heard the screen door screech open and saw Sarah waddling her way toward the swing.

Jenny held it still as Sarah eased her pregnant-self down to sit beside Jenny. Sarah held onto a cup of chamomile tea. Its relaxing aroma drifted over her and made Jenny smile, despite the weariness she felt inside.

She would have been better off if someone pulled out her heart, chewed it all up, then smashed it back in the center of her chest. At least then she would have a better excuse for why it hurt so much and why all she wanted to do was cry, lately.

Sarah set the swing to a gentle rock with her feet. She, nor her husband Michael, had said much about the accident. She was grateful for their friendship and understanding.

However, it was odd for Jenny to share her heartbreak and disappointments with Sarah. Usually it was the other way around.

Only Sarah had Michael now. She'd seen to that.

And while Jenny and Josh were twins, there were just some things a girl didn't share with her brother.

"Did you go again to the hospital today?" Sarah asked.

They hadn't spoken much at supper, except for listening to Sarah's son Ethan share about his day, and updates on the horses at the rescue and clinic.

Last year, when Sarah and Michael married, Michael's clinic and the rescue were also married together to become the Silver Wind Equine Rescue and Clinic.

"Yes, I went to see Mr. Sheridan today. He has a few broken ribs and some bruises. They're all surprised at the hospital that his injuries weren't worse than they are," Jenny said.

"Michael said the insurance adjuster called today. It'll take a few weeks to settle everything. The trucking company doesn't feel they have any fault in it since they didn't initiate the accident."

"This is all Brad's fault." Jenny slouched into the swing. In time she would forgive him, but right now the wound was too fresh. God forgive her that she could say the words of forgiveness with her mouth and not feel them in her heart.

"Why? Was Brad the one who was supposed to hitch the trailer?" Sarah asked.

"No. He was supposed to hitch *me*!" Suddenly, Jenny covered her mouth. *Had she really blurted that out?*

This was Sarah, and she knew what she said was safe with Sarah.

"I know your heart is broken right now. And I know that no matter what I say, it won't make you feel better right now. But I also know if it were me, you'd say 'everything happens for a reason and you just have to trust it's for the best.'"

Jenny giggled a little at hearing Sarah give her the same advice she always gives Sarah. "Like backing up to a trailer and forgetting to hitch it."

"I thought you said you got in and drove off?"

"I did. It never occurred to me that it wouldn't have been hitched since it was parked there like that. If Brad wouldn't have ..." Jenny fisted away the tears flooding her cheeks.

Sarah wrapped her arm around Jenny's shoulders. "There's no going back now. What's done is done."

For several minutes Jenny allowed herself to cry. If this is what she needed to get the raging emotions inside her to go away, then she'd let them out.

Sarah continued to rock and hold her as best friends do.

Finally, when she felt her tears ease and her chest lighten, Jenny sniffled and tried to wipe her damp face on her shirt sleeve.

"Feel better?" Sara asked as if she were talking to Ethan in her soothing mother-like voice.

"I don't think I'll feel better again," Jenny admitted. This was the first time since she was fifteen and Jake Huey had dumped her to go to the winter formal with Emma Delaney. She had felt crushed then, a mere drop in the bucket compared to having it shattered by Brad's omission.

"I understand what you're feeling. It will get better. I promise," Sarah said.

"I appreciate that, but it's not the same. Not like you and Michael. Brad already has a wife. It's not like I … We …"

"Jenny …" Sarah's tone of voice warned her not to go down that rabbit trail of thought.

But Jenny couldn't help it. Just a few days ago, she held onto hope for a future with the man she'd come to adore and felt she loved. Then in her most vulnerable moment, Brad had stabbed her in the heart with his deceit.

Jenny's throat tightened and her nose stung with the onset of another crying spell threatening to overwhelm her. She pressed her lips together and shook her head to ward it off.

"I can't." It came out as a mere whisper between her lips.

"Have you prayed about it?" Sarah's lips turned down and her eyes filled with concern for Jenny.

Had she prayed about it? Jenny almost snorted it. God was probably tired of listening to her pour out her grief and pain over it.

She even began to wonder if God wasn't sick of listening to her by now. Brad had, after all, called her a Bible thumper. One thing she wouldn't repeat or tell Sarah.

"I really thought he was going to ask me to marry him. How was I supposed to know, all this time, he had a wife and kids?"

Jenny's heart seized. She hugged herself, twisting her hands in the folds of her flannel shirt.

"Then this really is for the best. You don't want to spend the rest of your life with a man who would lie to you, would you?"

"He didn't lie. It's the truth that started this whole mess in the first place," Jenny recalled the words of Jesus in her mind. *Then you will know the truth and the truth will set you free.*

"Brad may not have lied to you with words, but he still got into a relationship with you knowing he was married. He deceived you."

Jenny couldn't argue. Sarah made a good point. It wasn't as if Jenny hadn't thought of it either, as she lay awake these past few nights.

She could never marry Brad. He had only gone to church on Sunday's in order to get closer to her. She knew that. Deep down she hoped by going to church it would change him—change his heart.

Somewhere she had failed him.

But it didn't stop her from missing him any less.

"Perhaps you need to find something to get your mind off all of this. Michael mentioned to me that if you'd like to take a few days off and go visit your parents or something, you can."

A few days off? That was the last thing she needed. More time to think about Brad. More time to replay the accident in her mind. More time to attend her own pity party. *No thank you!*

Sometime between coming out on the porch after supper and Jenny's crying spell, the sun had sunk below the horizon. A navy blur with spots of dark clouds gathered in the sky above the stables.

Inside, she could hear the sounds of music playing from one of Ethan's video games. Flashes of color from the television illuminated the window.

"It looks like Michael is done checking on the horses over at the clinic for the night," Sarah took a sip from the mug she'd been holding at her lap. From her wince, Jenny guessed her tea had gone cold.

"I guess that's my cue to head over to my place for the night," Jenny said.

A set of headlights glowed down the lane. Seeing Michael's truck was yet another reminder of the accident. Like Sarah said, "What is done is done," and now it was time for Jenny to pull herself together.

And to do so, she needed to do the right thing.

She needed to help Cade Sheridan.

It was the only way they would both be able to move on.

CHAPTER 5

The place was dark, except for the occasional blink of the old motel sign in the parking lot.

Someone moaned and someone whispered. His body froze in the open doorway. The heat from within blasted him like a furnace despite the August humidity at his back.

When the motel sign flashed, he saw her. Her long mane of blonde hair cascaded down her bare back, and when she looked at him, there was no shame in her eyes.

"Cade ..." his name escaped her lips, breathlessly.

"Well if that don't beat all ..." A male voice said, as the room went dark again.

Neither of them moved. Cade's hands turned into fists. His eyes never left his wife's face. Somewhere in the darkness, he heard the man rustling to get dressed. His shadow fell across the room as the motel sign blinked.

"I didn't think you'd be back so soon, pal."

He knew that voice.

"Cade, man ..."

He knew that voice all too well. "So is this your idea of sharing a motel, Dillon? To share a man's wife, too?"

"It's not like that, man. I swear. She ..." Dillon never got a change to finish his sentence. Cade hit him square in the jaw.

A scream ripped through the dark night as Dillon lunged at Cade and tackled him to the floor. He tried to push Dillon off, but the other man's weight knocked the breath from him.

"Stop it! Stop it!" Crystal screamed.

When Dillon looked up, Cade flipped him on his back and pinned him. A flash of light came through the doorway and the windows. Cade pounded his fists into Dillon's face until the other man's eyes rolled back.

He felt Crystal clawing at the back of his shirt.

Blood, dark like syrup, spread over Dillon's face.

Crystal yanked at his shoulder, hard. Cade paused. He stared down at Dillon's face.

She sobbed, tugging frantically at him. His gaze lifted to her face. Her hair, her glorious golden hair, was matted and its color muted in the darkness.

He reached out and smoothed his hand over her hair. She clung to his arm sobbing.

His hand fell away from her.

"Cade ...please ..." She sobbed.

In the distance he heard sirens.

He stood, letting Crystal fall across Dillon's body. She wept over him, her tears soaking his bare chest along with Dillon's blood.

Cade flexed his swollen fingers. Crystal looked up at him, wrapped in a sheet from the motel's bed.

There were two beds in the room. Why did she have to go crawling in DILLON's?

Sirens grew louder.

Cade turned; sweat beaded his forehead, trailing down the side of his face. Without a backward glance, he started walking.

She shouted his name.

After what seemed like one of the longest nights of her life, Jenny decided to take Michael up on his offer for a day or two off. Since she had a key to the equine clinic's office below her apartment, she spent her sleepless night putting things in order for the next day.

All the files for appointments were pulled and all the instructions Sarah would need to take care of Doc Miller and Michael for the day were laid out on the welcome desk.

Finally, at three in the morning, she dozed off in her desk chair with her head resting on her desk.

Around six-thirty, Michael came in like clockwork. She hadn't heard the jingle of the door, but when Michael pulled his iPad from out from under her, she jerked awake.

"I didn't mean to wake you. Just needed this." Michael held up the iPad.

Gingerly, Jenny stretched and came more fully awake. "There weren't any calls last night, so you're good to go."

He leaned forward on the counter above her desk. "Any reason you needed to pull an all-nighter?"

Jenny stood and pressed her hands into her back to stretch. Sleeping in a desk chair wasn't as comfy as her own bed, but at least for once in the days since the accident she had gotten some sleep.

"Yeah … about that …" She licked her dry lips and ran her hands through her hair. She needed a shower, and so far Michael hadn't said anything about her standing there in her lime green pajama shirt and black shorts.

"Sarah told you about taking a day off, did she?" There was a hint of humor in his voice, but his eyes were filled with the same kind of concern she'd seen in Sarah's eyes the night before.

"Do you mind? I mean if Sarah doesn't mind coming in? I'll help do the morning feedings and all. I have everything laid out and in order here for Doc's appointments while you're out on calls." Jenny claps her hand together, almost begging, almost in prayer for Michael to say yes.

He didn't disappoint her. "It'll have to be up to Sarah. I have to admit, I rather like the idea of knowing she'll be in here all day rather than stables where it's hot."

"Thank you."

Michael chuckled. "Don't thank me. You'll have to thank Sarah. Any chance there is coffee in the pot?"

Jenny walked out around from her desk. That's when Michael lifted an eyebrow when he saw her. She grinned and strolled back the hall to the supply room where they kept a coffee maker stashed with caffeine laced brew.

She had forgotten to program it the night before.

"Don't worry about it. Just go do what you need to do and I'll take care of this," Michael relieved her of the filter she grabbed.

Anxious to see Sarah, she headed for the door.

"You're at least going to change first, right?" Michael said.

She had almost forgotten she was still in her pajamas. "Oh, if you insist." She waved as she left.

Instead of finding Sarah in the barn, she spotted Josh cutting open a bale of hay.

"You're up early?" Jenny said.

"If I'm early, then you're late." Josh pulled the twine out from under the hay bale.

"You haven't gone to bed yet have you?" Jenny put a hand on her hip, but her brother didn't appear to have lost any sleep.

"Nope, but I'm heading out as soon as I'm done here to pick up a horse and take it to Lexington. I'd offer for you to ride along, but after hearing about your last trip on the highway I think I'm better of going solo."

"You only say that because you know I wouldn't go anyhow."

Josh grinned. He picked up a few chunks of hay and walked down the aisle. "Did you come to help or watch?"

Jenny grabbed a chunk of hay. "Where's Sarah?"

"Sleeping in, I suppose. I offered to switch with her this morning since I won't be back till late tonight." Josh shoved the hay into a nearby stall. A few of the horses nickered.

"Then I'll leave you to the task. I need to talk to Sarah."

"Now wait one minute." Josh paused from grabbing more chunks of hay. "Isn't it you who always says many hands make less work?"

Jenny smiled. "You'll have to credit Mom for that one, but I came out here to help Sarah so I can help you."

"Much obliged," Josh said in his best Texan drawl and tipped the brim of his ball cap.

Jenny's smile widened. "Which ones need let out?"

"Those three," Josh pointed behind her. "Just in the corral for today so Sarah can grab them this evening and put them back."

"Good idea." They didn't need Sarah hiking it out to one of the pastures to catch them and try leading them in. These three ponies were a handful ever since they gained some weight and realized they weren't tied to a pole that made them walk in circles anymore.

Jenny went over to one of their stalls. She grabbed a halter and a lead hanging on the hook by the stall door. A soft wrinkled muzzle met her as she slid open the door, eager for her to slip on its halter. This little gal's name was Sprinkles, because of her white coat and dark speckles of black through her coat. Like the other two beside her, Sprinkles had given hundreds of rides to children at birthday parties and fairs over the years. Each one tied to a pole, following each other, children were lifted on and off the saddle on her back, which had left an impression where her hair was worn off in places. This little pony's former owner never took the saddle off, over fed them enough grain, and hadn't trimmed their hooves for a long while, or so it appeared, when the Humane Society brought the trio to Silver Wind.

Jenny was able to gather and lead all three out of the stables. Sprinkles, and her two comrades Cupcake and Carmel, trotted side by side as she led them into the corral. Jenny couldn't get the leads off fast enough. Like kids, they ran and played and picked at each other in the warm morning sun.

When she returned, Josh had stashed the last of the hay in the stalls. He held out a pitch fork towards her. "Those stalls need cleaned."

Jenny hung up the leads and said, "Today's my day off."

Josh made a face showing his annoyance with her. "You're not running off with *him*, are you? Not after all the trouble he's caused."

Glad he was on her side for once, she shook her head. "Brad is long gone. Besides, I don't ever plan on speaking to him again."

"Good, cause if he ever comes back around here again, he'd have to go through me." Josh pulled the handle of the pitch fork close. It came as no surprise for her brother to want to protect her, and touched her at the same time.

"Have I ever told you that you're my favorite brother?" she asked.

"You mean your only brother," Josh said over his shoulder as he entered Sprinkle's empty stall.

"Exactly," Jenny said. "I have to get going; I still need to talk to Sarah before I head out."

"Just do me a favor. Don't go hooking up with some guy on the rebound. Trust me, it won't make you feel any better. Give yourself some time first."

She was taken aback by Josh's advice. She couldn't help wondering if that was what Josh had been doing this past year after Sarah rejected him and married Michael.

However, the last thing she needed right now was another man in her life, and she had no intention of wearing her heart on her sleeve anymore.

By the time she finished helping Josh at the rescue and was showered and ready to head to the hospital, her phone rang.

Jenny remembered when she first arrived at the hospital the morning after the accident, a nurse had questioned her about Cade. Since they had no contacts for him, the nurse seemed almost relieved she had come to visit him.

Now, after speaking with a nurse at the hospital, she felt giddy with her new self-appointed mission.

CHAPTER 6

"Mr. Sheridan?"

Suddenly, Cade's eyes flew open.

In his fist, he clutched his thin hospital blanket. Sweat poured down his face and soaked his back and pillow.

Baffled, he looked around the room. Someone had turned on the television and the curtain was pulled between the two beds. A waft of alcohol and bleach reminded him where he was.

"Mr. Sheridan?"

He turned his head in the direction of her voice. What was she doing here? He blinked and rubbed his eyes. She was still there. "It's you again."

"The hospital called and said you could go home today."

He clawed his fingers through his hair and took a deep breath. His dream had felt so real. Not like it happened more than a few years ago, but like the raw ache still clung to his ribs as if it happened this very morning.

He closed his eyes, willing it to all wash away from his mind. All the voices, the crying, the darkness, the surge of anger that flowed through his veins that night—it had been as if it was that night.

Only no one had spoken to him.

"Mr. Sheridan?"

"It's Cade, and what does me getting released today have anything to do with you? That is unless you brought me a new motorcycle."

Her lips twitched with a smile. She sat in the same chair as the day before with the same black leather Bible in her hands. Her hair was swept back with two little bronze barrettes.

"Unless you have someone else who can drive you, Mr. Sheridan. Um … Cade, you won't be leaving this hospital without me."

"Is that right?"

"I know I'm the last person you want to see right now, but from what you said yesterday, I'm guessing I'm all you got."

Cade laughed. "You just keep thinking that, sweetheart, but fact is I got plenty of others in line to take your place."

She leaned forward, leveled him with a piercing stare. "There's the phone. What are you waiting for?"

His gaze shifted to the punch button phone beside his bed. When he glanced back at her, she sat back in the chair with her arms folded and the Bible on her lap. Her upturned face smug with her eyes twinkling.

What was it any of her business if he had someone to call?

"A family member, your wife perhaps?" She chewed on her lower lip and scrunched her face. "Anybody?"

"I'm not married, but don't worry, you're off the hook. If you can just tell me where to find my saddle bags, I can take it from here."

Her face drained of its color.

If he hadn't been so annoyed with her, he might have been more sympathetic. "Everything I need is in my saddle bags."

Her lips curved down. She lowered her gaze to the Bible on her lap. There was no mistake, she prayed.

Suddenly, his chest ached and his throat constricted.

Did she pray for him?

He cleared his throat.

She glanced up. Two pink spots grew across her cheeks. She licked her lips and said, "I'm afraid they, too, were lost in the accident."

The accident *she* caused!

"I can take you and get you new ones."

"And everything in them?"

She bobbed her head in agreement.

"Then let's get going." Cade tossed back the covers.

Jenny gasped and looked away.

He chuckled, sat up, and winced. His breath came in a big gulp that he hissed to release. Pain shot up his left side and he clung to the metal rail of his bed.

Slowly, she peeked over at him. "Maybe I should go get a nurse."

"Yeah. You do that." It seemed like the only thing she was good at so far.

She leapt from the chair. The Bible hit the floor. She looked at it, then Cade, and then the Bible.

He arched an eyebrow.

She bent, picking up the Bible, tossing it on the end of the bed, and dashed from the room like a calf released out of the chute.

A set of hooves hitting him square in the chest would have felt better than the dull ache of his ribs. Cade insisted on dressing himself and there was no way they were carting him out of here in one of those wheel chairs.

He could walk, and by his own two feet, would he walk out of here.

Except for the fact, he had yet to figure out how he was going to get his boots on. He'd tried stepping a foot down into them, but every time he reached down to pull the boot up and shove his heel down, the pain of his ribs shot up his sides and caused him to howl. He sounded worse than a coyote on the prairie.

"I can help you with that."

He looked up from staring down at his half-booted foot. "I can do it myself."

"If you say so."

In a matter of a few hours, this tearful apologetic sapling of a woman had transformed into a cocky know it all. He couldn't say he liked the know-it-all-type. He just wanted to get out of here. He just wanted to get his ride back.

He gave up on getting his boot on. There was nothing wrong with letting a woman put on a man's boots. Crystal had helped him a time or two, but that thought alone stung a new burr into his side.

"If you don't mind ..."

"I don't." She tossed her handbag on the bed and bent down to his boot. His face grew hot as he gazed down at her on her knees. She gripped the top of his boot and he pushed his foot the rest of the way inside.

Who would have known that something so simple as lifting his leg would cause a pinch in his side?

"Ready for the next one?"

Her hair lay in jagged layers to the side and the back was spiked. He wasn't one for liking short hair on a woman, but it looked good on her. Too good.

She hiked up the boot and his heel slammed inside. He winced.

"Oh, did that hurt?" she asked.

He grimaced.

"Ready?" She grabbed her handbag.

"Yeah, I'm so happy to get out of here I don't care where you take me." He wrapped an arm around his ribs and limped from the hospital room. She reached for him, but Cade shrugged her off.

"Aren't you forgetting something?" Cade asked.

When Jenny stared at him blankly, he pointed to the Bible she had left on the end of his hospital bed.

"Nope. As lovely as it is, that Bible stays here. It goes in the drawer of the bedside table you were using."

Cade grunted and headed for the door.

Silently, Jenny trailed behind him. At the nurses' station, two nurses rose and came around the corner. "You just wait right there, Mr. Sheridan, while we get you a wheelchair."

"I won't need that. Thank you just the same." He continued limping toward the elevator at the end of the hall.

One nurse ran down the hall while another jumped in front of Cade. Jenny walked beside him "Now just a minute Mr. Sheridan. I can't let you walk out of here."

Jenny walked up beside the elevator and leaned against the wall.

"Says who?"

When the nurse peered around him Cade turned. Nurse Jim came strolling down the hallway with a wheelchair.

He looked back at the nurse, and then at Jenny. She bit her lip and turned her face away, but he saw she laughed at him.

"Please, Mr. Sheridan, it's hospital policy."

Cade held his aching ribs and took an unsteady breath. He looked into the nurse's pleading eyes and sighed. She smiled and took hold of his arm as Jim pushed the wheelchair up behind him. Cade eased himself back into the wheelchair. He shifted his gaze toward Jenny while the nurse set his legs in the metal footrests. Jenny lost her bemused look.

Jim pushed him forward and Cade winked at the nurse, who blushed when she backed away from him in the hall. Jenny rolled her eyes and pressed the button for the elevator. "Do you always refuse help when offered?"

"I'm in the chair, aren't I?" Cade said, as Jim pushed him inside the elevator. Jenny stepped in beside them.

No one said a word as the elevator went down.

She scowled at him as the elevator doors slid open.

As soon as Jim pushed him out on to the main level, Cade put the brakes on. "I can walk from here."

Jim put his hands up. "Gotta walk out to impress the girl, huh? Don't sweat it, Bud. You're on your own now."

Jim walked around and held out his hand to help Cade, but Cade already had his feet to the floor and in one hurried motion propelled himself out of the chair. Fire shot up his side. His breath hissed through his teeth.

Jim handed Jenny a bunch of papers and gave her instructions. Cade waited for the fire to ease in his ribs.

"Are you sure you don't want that wheel chair?" Jenny asked.

"Why? You in a hurry to unload me somewhere?" Cade limped past her.

"I just thought it might be easier for you in your current state."

Cade stopped and stared at her. "Current state?'

"You know the limp, the broken ribs ... You just got out of the hospital."

Cade looked around. "It doesn't look like I'm out of here yet."

"You've got two feet to go, shall we?" She held out her hand in the direction of the sliding glass doors. "My car is parked in front."

"While I appreciate that, it would have been easier for me getting in a truck."

She paled. "The truck was in use today, but I'll remember that for the next time."

As far as Cade was concerned, there would be no next time.

Outside the hospital, she led him to a little blue coupe sedan. She unlocked the door and held it open for him.

"I believe it should be I who is doing that for you."

"This isn't a date," Jenny said, gripping the door.

Cade slid down into the cloth interior seat and looked up at her. "Doesn't mean a man can't still open a door for a lady."

Jenny shoved the door shut and walked around to the driver's side. Once she settled behind the driver's wheel, she turned and looked at him. Cade stared back. For a long moment, their eyes locked and he knew if he didn't look away, he'd forget the last 48 hours. "So what, we just sit here?"

"You forgot your seat belt." Her hand was poised on the key in the ignition.

Cade reached for his seat belt and pain shot through his side. He jerked his hand back as if he had been burnt.

"No can do." He took a few short breaths waiting for the pain to ease.

"Maybe you shouldn't be leaving here so soon," Jenny said.

Cade didn't doubt she was right, but he wasn't about to stay laid up in a hospital bed one more day. He had places to go and people who were expecting him.

"Changed your mind already, have you?" he asked.

Jenny titled her chin up. "I just want to make sure you're all right."

"Well, you can put your conscience at rest. Now, if you don't mind, I'd like to get going." He tried once more to buckle his seatbelt, and the same pain prevented him. He hissed through his teeth.

"Hold still," she unbuckled her belt and reached over him. Her soft hair brushed his cheek as she grabbed his seat belt and pulled it across him. He drank in the sweet smell of apple blossoms and closed his eyes.

He heard the belt buckle click and then looked at her. She turned the key and praise music blared inside the car. Quickly, she switched off the radio.

"Saddle bags, remember? And I could use a good sharp razor." He rubbed the stubble on his chin.

CHAPTER 7

It didn't take long before she pulled into the Shelbyville Wal-Mart parking lot. "I doubt they have saddle bags, but we can replace all your other stuff here."

The parking lot was packed with mid-morning shoppers. Jenny parked next to a handicap spot and reached over toward Cade's seat belt clip.

She halted mid-reach at the sound of his seatbelt unbuckling. She got out, walked around, and opened the car door for him. His face contorted, he didn't complain this time. He swung one leg out and then the other. Ignoring her stretched hand, he pulled himself out of the passenger seat and stood.

As if she were assisting her eighty-year-old grandmother, Jenny took Cade by the arm.

He glanced down at her hand. "It's not my arms that are broken."

"You just got out of the hospital."

"You keep reminding me of that. Yet, it's not the first time, either."

She didn't know if that was supposed to make her feel better, but it most defiantly did not.

Leaning to the left, Cade limped across the parking lot. He

bent his arm and clutched his ribs. To a passerby they might have appeared as a couple.

She didn't want to think about couples. Not now, not while she carried the grief of loving a married man on her chest, like a horse pulling a plow.

Jenny glanced down at Cade's hands. They were bare with a bit of road rash spread up from his wrist to his forearm where his jacket must have pushed up at the sleeve during the accident.

"Here, I'll get a cart," she said, relieved for the distraction.

Cade limped behind her.

"Oh good, I was afraid they would all be in use. You can ride in this while we shop." She pointed out the motorized cart with a seat.

Cade lifted a brow. "I think I'd prefer to walk if you don't mind."

By the look on his face, she decided not to argue. She pulled out a regular cart and waited for him. He limped over and took the cart, slowly pushing it through the store's entrance.

She followed, and when Cade headed into the men's department, she pulled clothes from the racks.

"Listen, I'm sure you've got other things you need to do."

"Nope. I took time off today so I could help you." Jenny held up a blue plaid button down shirt. "How about this one?"

Cade looked at the shirt, then at her. "I know what you're trying to do and I appreciate it, but I don't need your help. I don't need your sympathy. And I don't need you picking out my clothes."

"How about this one?" She held out the same shirt in red. "I think you look better in blue."

She tossed the shirt in the cart. The sooner she helped Cade, the sooner she'd accomplish that mission she'd appointed herself.

Cade rested his forearms on the cart handle and bent his head, still watching her. "Are you going to pick out my underwear too?"

"Men's underwear is all the same, there's not much to choose from." She turned and resumed her search at the shirt rack.

"I'm not sure a girl like you should be sorting through another man's clothes."

Jenny felt her spine stiffen. "What do you mean, 'a girl like me'?"

"We wouldn't want your boyfriend finding a pair of men's underwear in your hands, now would you?"

Jenny gasped. She whirled around and faced him. "What makes you think I'm *that* type of girl or that I even have a boyfriend?"

Cade coughed.

Jenny's cheeks grew hot. "I didn't mean … I-I'm not …."

"Of course not." Cade clutched his right side.

"What's that supposed to mean?"

Cade shrugged. "I don't know. You tell me."

"I'll have you know that I have a—." But she couldn't complete her sentence. Brad wasn't her boyfriend. Not anymore.

"What do you have?" Cade asked, looking confused.

She thought for a moment and said, "A horse. I have a horse."

"A horse?"

"Yeah, a bunch actually. I help run Silver Wind Equine Rescue and Clinic."

"For a minute there, I thought you were going to say you were married."

Jenny forced herself to smile. "It's hard to get married when you don't have a boyfriend."

"That's right. Whole reason we're here isn't it? Woman, your love life nearly killed me!"

"Basically."

"Can't say I'm sorry for your loss," he said.

"It was Brad's fault, really. If he would have proposed instead of forcing me to have to dump him like that, I would have never run into you."

"Lucky me." Cade pushed the cart further into the men's department.

"I'm glad you understand."

Cade reached for a pair of Wrangler's and paused mid-reach. Jenny snatched the denim pants from the shelf and handed them to him. Spotting the size, she sorted through another pile trying to find one more pair.

She tried to stay back, only assisting him when he couldn't reach. Brad would have talked about underwear with her. Unlike Cade, Brad always treated her with respect and kindness. That's what she loved about him most.

Not that Cade could understand. He was lucky all right. Lucky she came to see him or the hospital wouldn't have had anyone else to call for his discharge. What kind of man didn't have a family to call?

They came to the cash register and she piled Cade's items onto the register belt. Cade pulled out his wallet, but Jenny was quicker. She swiped her card through the reader before Cade could stop her.

He waited until they were back out in the parking lot and said, "You didn't have to do that."

"Yes, I did. I just wouldn't feel right knowing that you lost all your stuff without replacing it for you. At least you'll have clean clothes and a razor to shave until you get home."

At the car, Jenny dug into her bag for keys. "I'll just put my stuff in here." Cade said, reaching down in the cart for a brand new black duffel bag. That alone had been almost half their shopping bill.

Wal-Mart didn't sell saddlebags as she suspected. Just as well, or it would have put a bigger dent in her credit card.

"I've got it. You get in." Jenny set the duffel bag atop the car trunk and loaded it with the bags of clothes and toiletries.

"Thanks." Cade shifted as he stood there watching her zip the bag closed.

"It's the least I can do."

"Just one more thing," Cade said.

"What's that?"

"Can you drop me off at the nearest bus station? I don't suppose you have a phone on you, do you?"

"You do have someone to call!" Jenny grinned.

"I'm supposed to be in Augusta by Friday."

Jenny's grin turned upside down. "That's the day after tomorrow."

"That's why I need a phone."

"But you're in no condition to travel that far," Jenny said.

"Nor do I have a place to stay, either."

She took a deep breath and without even stopping to pray about it, said, "Then I'm taking you to Silver Wind. There's a phone and a place for you to stay. I'll drive you to Augusta tomorrow if you still need to get there."

"Thanks, but I think you've done enough."

"Get in this car. I'm taking you home with me." Jenny tossed the duffel bag in the back seat of the car, giving him no choice. She set out this morning determined to help him and help him she would.

Cade reached for the passenger side door handle. "I guess if you put it that way."

"I hope you like pot roast, because that's what's on the menu tonight."

CHAPTER 8

They turned down an old country road. Cade gazed out at the green fields sweltering in the hot Kentucky sun.

The last thing Cade expected was for Jenny to offer him a place to stay. It was the pain medication dulling his mind; otherwise, never in his right mind would he have agreed.

If he hadn't already figured out the motivation behind Jenny's offer, she'd made it clear to him in the store. Bringing him here was just one more way for her to clear that pretty little head of hers about the accident.

At the crossroads, she turned right. He spotted a large house and barn with a huge sign in front of the lane. "Silver Wind Equine Rescue and Clinic, uh?"

"Like I told you, this is where I work. The clinic is across the road here. You'll be staying in the cottage house with my brother, Josh."

He thought about asking where she stayed, but decided against it. He didn't want her thinking this was anything more than what it was. He'd slept in more peculiar places than this, and his aching ribs reminded him a soft bed was better than a hay bale and metal floor for the night, like back in his rodeo days.

As they pulled into the lane past the clinic, he spotted a small carriage house on the left of the lane. "A motel would have worked just fine."

If she heard his comment, she ignored him. She parked in front of the cottage house. "Supper is at the farm house down the lane. You're on your own for lunch. There's food in the fridge, so you can help yourself. If you need a lift getting to the farmhouse just call over to the clinic, the number is written on the paper by the wall."

"And your brother isn't going to mind me crashing in on him?"

"Josh comes in for supper and crashes here to sleep, most days he's on the road delivering or picking up horses and cattle for local farmers." She got out of the car and walked around to the passenger side. Before she had a chance, Cade opened the door and swung his legs out. She waited for him before heading around back to grab his bag.

She led him to the front door and as she flicked the keys in her hand. Cade relieved her of his new belongings.

Jenny smiled as she unlocked the door and pushed it open for him to enter. They walked into a small living area and she point-ed. "Josh's room is over there on the left. There's a spare room to the right, so you shouldn't disturb each other."

She headed into the kitchen, opening the fridge, she frowned. Looking around at the flannel shirt thrown across the couch and the dirty dishes piled in the sink, she decided not to stick around long enough to have to play housemaid to roommate.

"Supper's at six." Then she turned and left him at the front door of the empty cottage. "Remember to call the clinic if you need anything."

He waited to hear the door shut before he made his way to the spare bedroom. He tossed his bag on the bed and pulled out the bottle of pain medication the doctor prescribed and filled for him at the hospital. He debated walking back to the kitchen then swallowed the pill dry. Putting the bottle down on the bedside table, he eased himself onto the bed's patchwork quilt. Exhaust-ed, he fell asleep as soon as his head touched the pillow.

Back inside the clinic Jenny found Mrs. Miller at the reception desk. "You're back sooner than we thought. Take care of that fellow of yours?"

"He's not my fellow, Mrs. Miller," Jenny said, wondering where Sarah was. When Jenny left this morning Sarah reassured her she'd stepped in to cover here at the clinic.

"Oh I know," Mrs. Miller nodded waved off the notion. "Although another man called for you while you were gone. Sweetest voice should have been a country singer."

Jenny's heart beat faster. "Did you get his name and number?"

Doc Miller's wife turned an extra shade of pink as she reached for the slip of paper and handed it to Jenny. "Said his name was Brad."

Jenny took the slip of paper and stared at the number. She couldn't talk to him. Not now. Not ever. With Mrs. Miller on the other side of the receptionist desk and a few people glancing her way as they talked, memories of the last time Brad came strutting through those doors rehashed. She crumbled the paper in her fist.

She wouldn't think about Brad. It was over, and once she finished helping Cade, they both would be able to move on. Hopefully, sooner rather than later.

A hot gust of air swept into the waiting room as an elderly woman came in with her Dachshund on a leash.

Quickly, she stuffed the crumbled paper into her back pocket.

"Maggie Shell, well I'll be!" Mrs. Miller said as she spotted the elderly woman entering the clinic

This was a good time for Jenny to relieve Mrs. Miller of the receptionist desk. If she had to guess, Sarah was back over at the rescue or with Michael.

Mrs. Miller had been coming to the clinic more often than not, it seemed. "I've got this, Dear. Why don't you head over to the rescue and give Sarah a hand?"

Jenny didn't know what to say at Mrs. Miller's suggestion. She wasn't so certain this was a good idea. She'd seen Mrs. Miller's records from when Doc Miller had been running things in town on his own. Michael moved here to take over Doc's practice and expand his dream of an equine clinic, but Doc wasn't ready for retirement and stayed on taking care of the clinic's smaller animal patients.

It was getting harder for Sarah to care for the horses in her condition. With Jenny at the clinic and Josh always away for his hauling business, they were becoming short-handed with the number of horses they had accumulated lately.

Jenny knew she should be grateful, so she said, "Thank you for helping us today, Mrs. Miller."

"I'd forgotten how wonderful it was to see people every day. Some days are kind of lonely with Ivan here and the girls are all grown now with little ones of their own." Mrs. Miller kept an eye on Mrs. Shell coming towards them.

"Did you understand our scheduling and billing system alright then?" Jenny asked.

"We never had a computer, you can't delete paper."

That was what Jenny was afraid of hearing. "I could show you. It's really simple."

Mrs. Miller seemed to ponder Jenny's suggestion. "I don't know. I'd like to come and help out once in a while. Mind you, I am retired now."

"Of course." Jenny smiled. She could tell the older woman's eyes shone with excitement at the offer.

"I've got the folder and the times wrote on them for me to keep track. I suppose learning to use that machine would work better for keeping the appointments straight rather than having two appointment books, wouldn't it?" Mrs. Miller was watching Mrs. Shell pick up her little dog as she spoke.

"I can show you now, if you'd like." Jenny moved to come around the desk.

Mrs. Shell came up to stand behind her.

"Oh no, you don't," Mrs. Miller gently pushed Jenny back. "I got my system right here for today." She picked up a file folder for Mrs. Shell's dog, Pepper. "You go on now, and we'll save the lessons for another day. Sarah's waiting."

Reluctantly, Jenny stepped back. As she went to point at the computer, Mrs. Miller waved her off. "You can go in tomorrow and fix it on your computer there, but for now I've got a patient waiting to sign in for an appointment." Mrs. Miller turned her attention from Jenny to Mrs. Shell and Pepper. "Isn't that right, Pepper?"

The Dachshund yipped in response. Mrs. Miller reached over and petted the dog on the head.

"He's in need of his shots again," Mrs. Shell said.

"Is that so? Well, I'll be sure to have a treat for him when he's done. I do believe there are some doggie treats around here somewhere," Mrs. Miller said.

"In the drawer to your left." Jenny went to reach for it when Mrs. Miller slapped her hand away.

Jenny opened her mouth, but Mrs. Miller arched her brow. She let her hand drop and turned away. When old Doc Miller had told her about his missus having treats for the animals after shots or stitches, Jenny had made up special treat bags for their four-legged patients.

As Mrs. Miller and Mrs. Shell caught up with one another, Jenny made her way out of the clinic. She wondered if offering to show Mrs. Miller how to use the computer had been such a good idea after all. What would happen to her if Mrs. Miller decided to spend more and more time behind the reception desk?

She chided herself. Michael wouldn't allow it. Especially since she routed his appointments, took care of the billing, and coordinated the equine facility.

This would, however, give her a chance to help the rescue more and help Sarah. Maybe Josh had enough business hauling that she could borrow Michael's truck and trailer … Suddenly, she cringed. Perhaps it was the sound of truck tires crunching on the gravel parking lot. Either way, it made her think of Cade's accident and how long before Michael would trust her to drive his truck and trailer again.

From now on, she made a mental note to be sure to check if things were hitched before she took off with them, men included.

CHAPTER 9

Cade hung up the phone with his client in Augusta. He hoped this set back didn't cost him any more jobs in addition to his motorcycle.

He stepped out of the stable's office into the shade of the barn aisle. Sweat powered down his forehead and his back. He tugged at his shirt to relieve it from sticking. For late afternoon, the humidity still clung to the breeze. His excursion from walking this far caused him to break out in a sweat. Having been laid up in the hospital those few days had made him lazy.

He tugged at his t-shirt to relieve it from sticking and leaned against the first stall.

Most of the horses were out in the fields. He heard the rustle down the row and limped towards it. Just then, Jenny walked out from around the corner. She stood in front of a stall door and pulled a carrot out from the back pocket of her jeans.

She hadn't seen him standing there. Cade stayed back, catching his breath, and watching the curvy red head as she spoke to the horse within.

"Gee, I'm happy to see you, too." She laughed, a seductive sound, causing Cade to want to inch closer to her.

"I guess I should have seen that coming. I have a habit, you know, of running men off or over lately." Jenny leaned against the stall door and spoke through the bars as if she were in a confessional.

Cade didn't want to intrude, so he remained a few stalls back, but he couldn't help but listen to her sad husky voice as she spoke to the horse.

"He called. Left a message at the clinic. Even if he called to say that he wasn't married, which I don't know because I am not calling him back. I don't know if I could believe him. My heart keeps telling me this isn't true. But I know it is. I've tried talking to Sarah, but she doesn't understand, even though she says she does. How could she? She's always been in love with Michael."

From within the stall, the horse blew hard through its nostrils.

"What? My love life depresses you?" Jenny held out the carrot through the bars. "At least I have a love life ... or *had* one."

Inside, the horse didn't respond. Jenny waved the carrot up and down. "Come on. It's a carrot. It's food." Jenny pulled back the carrot, pretended to chew on it and then thrust it back between the metal bars.

Cade bit his lip from chuckling.

She sighed after a minute, pulling the carrot back again. "You know if you tried it, you might like it."

She tried again, but the horse didn't take the carrot. She walked back around the corner and Cade moved closer. Curious, he wanted to see what Jenny's friend looked like.

She returned with an apple in hand. "You're the stubbornest horse I've ever met."

A horse muzzle reached out toward her hand, its lips twitching for the apple.

Jenny reached in. He heard the crunch of the hard fruit, and as she withdrew her empty hand, he bumped against a rake leaning against the next stall door.

She looked over as he tried to reach for the rake before it fell. "Cade."

Jenny lurched forward for it at the same time as he did. They both held on to it.

"I see you found the barn. How long have you been here?" She tried to pull the rake handle in her direction.

"Not long. Was on my way to the house," Cade said.

Relief spread over her face. Or was it that she was annoyed with him? He could never tell with women.

In the midst of horse dung and hay, he could still catch a whiff of her perfume – flowery and sweet.

He reached up with his free hand to swipe away the sweat from his forehead while his stomach reminded him of the reason he left the cottage in the first place.

There was nothing in the fridge that hadn't expired or appeared like a science experiment that he was willing to try. With little choice and no cash in his wallet, he couldn't order delivery. So the main house it was.

"I got this." Jenny tugged on the rake.

Cade couldn't bring himself to let go. "I'll take care of it."

"I got it out. I was about to put it away anyhow," Jenny said.

"Just tell me where it goes."

Jenny's eyes narrowed on him. "I got it out. I'll put it away."

Her lips thinned into a tight line as she looked at him. If she hadn't been the one to cause him to wreck his motorbike, he might have thought that expression of hers cute, but she did and he wasn't planning on sticking around any longer than necessary. "Have it your way."

Cade loosened his hold on the rake and she yanked it from him. "If you wait a second, I'll walk up to the house with you."

"For a moment there I thought you were going to offer to take me up in your chariot."

By the glare he received from her, she didn't appear amused. She put the rake back into a supply stall as Cade limped closer to her horse friend. A buckskin stallion shied away from him.

"Hello there," Cade measured the animal's response to him.

"He's name is Apple," Jenny said.

"Apple?" Now that was an interesting name for a horse, Cade

thought.

"He only eats apples."

"Is that a fact?" Cade peered in at the buckskin. The stallion appeared a bit on the thin side. "Looks like he wouldn't hurt to gain a pound or two rather than slim him down anymore."

"You tell that to him."

"You need some oats, Boy," Cade said to the horse.

"Trust me, he's got enough wild oats in him for the entire lot we have here."

"Have you tried molasses in his oats?"

"We've tried everything. He'll eat hay, grass, and apples. And not even the apple horse treats. He picks them out of his feed and drops them. His feed always goes untouched."

"Teeth?"

"Michael says he's fine. Besides, are you going to tell me you're an expert on horses?"

Cade shrugged. "Been breaking them since I was fifteen."

"Well, Apple here has already had it pretty rough. That's why he's here at the rescue. We're praying in time he will settle down and we'll be able to find him a good home."

Somehow, by the sound of her lowering voice, Cade didn't feel Jenny was all too eager to see that happen.

She headed out of the barn and Cade followed her. He glanced back over his shoulder at the stallion then back at Jenny. "A bit dangerous having an untamed stallion in the barn here, isn't it?"

Jenny shrugged.

So that was the way of it. "Anyone working with him?"

"He's settled down a lot since he first came. We're just not able to turn him out with the other horses, and he's not a people horse." Jenny slowed as he limped to catch up with her.

"That's not what I asked."

"You offering? I thought you were leaving soon."

"I am," Cade said.

"Then it makes no difference," Jenny said.

A screen door opened and a Beagle dog rushed out to the front yard. "Ellie, here Ellie." Jenny called the dog to her. It jumped up and she crouched down to give it attention.

Cade limped past her to the porch. A pregnant woman greeted him from behind the screen door. "Hi there. I'm Sarah Wolfe and you must be Cade Sheridan."

"I appreciate your hospitality," Cade said.

"It's the least we can do. I hope you like pot roast," Sarah said.

"My favorite," Jenny came from behind Cade and slipped in the house past Sarah. "Any chance of brownies for dessert?"

Sarah Wolfe gave him an apologetic smile and pushed open the screen door wider motioning for him to come in. "Come on in. Michael's taken Ethan out on a call, so it's just the three of us for supper tonight."

"Josh isn't back yet?" Jenny asked from inside.

"He seems to eat on the run lately," Sarah said over her shoulder before looking at Cade. "If you want any of that dessert, you'd best come in before Jenny finds it." Sarah motioned for Cade to follow her down the hall to the kitchen.

The last thing on Cade's mind was warm chocolate.

CHAPTER 10

The next day, Jenny found herself scrolling through the online classified ads in search for a motorcycle. She'd made herself a list during the night: Since Cade was staying at the cottage; he currently had a place to stay. Now, all he needed was a new motorcycle. She'd heard him tell Sarah at supper that he had six weeks to kill until he was due at his next job, but six weeks was far too long in her mind. She was determined to get Cade back on the road and headed back to his life, before the accident, sooner rather than later—for both their sakes.

She punched the down arrow on her keyboard, this time a little harder than the last.

The office was quiet this afternoon. Doc Miller left an hour ago, and Michael was due back from his rounds any minute. She expected him to arrive the same time as a new racehorse being admitted to the clinic with a fractured femur.

She heard the jingle of the bell over the door and quickly minimized the classified page on her screen.

Josh ambled inside, his pants caked with fresh manure and his long sleeved thermal shirt torn on one corner.

"What happened to you?" Jenny got up and stood at the corner of her desk.

Josh wiped the sweat from brow with his shirtsleeve. "Tell Michael the stalls are clean; you'll have to take care of feeding tonight."

A trickle of blood ran down Josh's upper lip from his nose. Jenny grabbed a tissue off the desk and rushed over to him before he could wipe the blood with his shirtsleeve.

He flinched and tried to push her way, "I don't need you to wipe my nose. You're not my mother."

Taken back, Jenny let Josh take the tissue from her hand and stepped away to put some distance between them. She saw, then, the dark bruise on the side of his cheek bone. His hairline was socked with sweat and his eyes were bloodshot.

"Josh?" Her voice quivered, but remained stern. "What happened?"

Josh took a big step around her and dodged her question as he snatched several more tissues.

"Josh?" she said, this time sterner, fear pushing her adrenaline level and making her heart race.

"I stepped on a pitch fork." Josh stuffed the end of the tissues in the side of his nose to try to stop the bleeding. It had been bleeding before. A dark smudge stained the back of his shirt sleeve.

"A pitch fork?" Part of her felt relieved that he hadn't gotten into a tussle with one of the horses. A few of the clinic horses belonged to the rescue and were being housed in the clinic's stables while receiving treatment. Josh knew better than to turn his back on these estranged animals.

"Yeah, I tilted it up against the wall and went to get a load of sawdust. When I came back the pitch fork was gone, so I thought I had put it somewhere else. Low and behold I take a step forward and it had fallen into the lose hay and I stepped on it." His voice trembled and she could tell by the pitch of his voice he was angry.

"It hit you in the nose." She sighed, "Come on, there's an ice pack in the break room and some Tylenol."

Josh shook his head, "I got to go. I've got two horses to pick up down on the other side of town and take down to Mayfield tonight."

"What about the horse in Lexington? You know the one that Dad called you about?" Jenny remembered her mother mentioning their father had called Josh about a possible surrendered horse that had been abandoned after it lost its last three races. The owner had left it at the track, and a friend of her father had asked if Silver Wind could pick up the horse and find it a new home.

"I'll get it later this week. Knowing Mom, I'll be expected to stop in at the house." Josh pulled out the tissue, satisfied the bleeding had stopped, and he tossed it into the waste basket by Jenny's desk.

"Mom did say Dad would look after it till you got it. We could ride up together on Sunday."

"I ain't staying for church," Josh said. "I might show up for dinner, but if Mom makes meatloaf –no thank you."

Jenny took a deep breath. In the past year, Josh had been drifting away from attending church services and now he seemed to avoid Sunday dinners with their parents. Mom made meatloaf and mash potatoes every Sunday and she, like Josh, knew that would never change.

"I thought you like sitting by Kristy Johnson during service." Jenny smiled sweetly at him.

"I think you and Kristy Johnson have been hanging out together too much, she's starting to act like you," Josh said.

"What do you mean, act like me?" She put her hands on her hips.

"Oh come on Jenny, everybody knows you're a Bible Thumper."

That was what Brad had called her! She turned away and grabbed a tissue of her own. She waited, waited, for her brother to wrap his arm around her shoulders and tell her he didn't mean it, but then she heard, "Well I've got to go. I'll catch you later."

She listened as his boots clicked across the wood floor and the bell jingled above the door as he left. *Bible Thumper.* Is that what people really thought of her? *Was it true Lord? Was she really a Bible Thumper?*

She decided, as she sat back down at her desk, that the first thing she would do is Google "Bible Thumper."

CHAPTER 11

Cade stood at the old stone bridge, watching the water swirl and rush down the small stream. It would be a long hot summer should they not get a drop of rain soon.

He gazed out over the property. The old stone house he figured held generations of history. The U-shaped stables gleamed of new paint, white with green trim. It was the bridge which captured his attention and drew him forward in a slow pace.

He admitted, going to supper in the old stone house made him drag his feet. However, he wasn't sure a can of cold beans from the cupboard or a frozen dinner would satisfy his hunger.

This bridge reminded him of one out of the storybooks his mother used to read him. He couldn't remember his mother ever sitting long enough to read a book to the finish. There were always chores to do in the house, out in the barn, and especially in the summer when there were weeds to pull from the garden.

There was no place for weeds in his mother's garden. She'd rip out the ones that choked and ensnared the fruitful plants. Cade was one of those weeds. He'd cut himself free from her apron strings long ago.

The sounds of trickling water made him stop and admire the wooden wheel cranking slowly through the creek. Attached to the wheel, an old carriage house that had become his temporary home. Home, he hadn't really had one of those in a long time.

He stuffed his hands in his pockets. Wouldn't his mother just smile to see a view like this? Maybe he'd take a picture and send it to her. He may not still be a part of the pumpkin patch these days, but he let his mother know he was still alive once in a while with a letter. Seldom did he ever call, so that he would not have to hear her crying at the end of the line when he said goodbye.

He crossed the bridge. There didn't seem to be anyone around. They were probably all at the house.

A few days ago, he would have laughed if someone had told him he would end up exactly where he'd started. He was tempted to take his supper with the horses, but was afraid molasses and oats wouldn't settle well with his stomach. Nevertheless, he headed for the stables.

Cade stepped into the dim interior of the stables' walk way. Light shone from inside the office, and he frowned. Around the doorway, he spied Jenny. A soft sigh escaped her lips. She sat staring at a computer screen with a stack of papers at her left elbow.

He leaned against the doorway and smiled. Her eyes seemed weary, the little fire that could burn through a man's soul, had been extinguished. It had been a long day for all of them.

Yet, his heart pinched in his chest at the sight of her damp pale cheeks. Since when did he care about someone else's sorrows? Plenty of women he had known cried over the dumbest things, but not this one.

What had happened to drench the fire within those eyes? His mother would have quoted Philippians, "I can do all things through him who strengthens me."

He stood watching her, amazed that after all these years he could still remember that verse.

The small office had all the standard equipment, but the desk and filing cabinet had seen better days. The wood plank walls remained plain and empty. He didn't imagine this place brought in much money, being non-profit and all.

He could have cared less about the insurance check for the motorcycle, had that motorcycle not been his only set of wheels.

But funny as it seemed, he wasn't in any hurry to hightail it out of here, as he had all the other places he'd been. After years on the road, he never could settle in just one place.

He must have shifted, making a sound, because Jenny looked up.

She patted her cheeks dry with her shirt sleeve. "I didn't realize anybody else was here."

"By the look on your face, I'd say you were hoping I was someone else."

Jenny tilted her head and tried to smile, but her bottom lip quivered. "You get used to it after a while," she said.

When he seemed lost for a reply she continued by saying, "The someone else part. You're either second best or not good enough at all."

Cade crossed his arms, "I take it he was a real jerk."

"Who?"

"The guy who dumped you."

But that didn't make her smile. If anything the little flame in her eyes ignited. "I dumped him."

"I can see how that would be upsetting enough that you would nearly kill a man," Cade regretted his words as soon as he said them.

If her face hadn't been pale before, her complexion turned ghostly white. "I- I ... How was I supposed to know the trailer wasn't hitched? It was an accident!"

"Most people make sure they're hitched before they drive off," Cade said.

Jenny's chin notched up a degree higher. She pushed back from her seat at the desk and stood. They looked one another in the eyes for a long moment before she said, "I think I hear a truck coming down the lane. That'll be Michael coming home for supper. If you'd like, I'll help you to the house with that bum leg of yours."

"I've been getting around just fine with this bum leg of mine for quite some time now, thank you just the same," Cade said.

From down the aisle a horse screamed and chaos broke loose. Jenny dashed past Cade as they both headed into the aisle way. A blur of beige and black came barreling toward them.

CHAPTER 12

Cade half ran, half hopped, to the entrance and grabbed the stable door and pulled. Jenny didn't move. She nearly toppled over as the wild stallion zoomed past her and headed for the door. Cade yanked as hard as he could and the sliding door banged shut. The stallion reared back on both hind legs and kicked his front feet at the door. Cade backed away from the flying hooves.

Jenny spun around. "Get out of there!"

There was nothing he could do. He'd backed himself in a corner. The stallion spun in circles kicking at the door, just inches from Cades' shoulder. Cade took a deep breath and reached out toward the horse's halter. Behind him, Jenny waved her hands, "Get out of there. Go back to your stall," but by her quivering voice, he knew she was afraid. So did the stallion.

The stallion spun around. His nostrils flared wide. He shook his head and bared his teeth toward Jenny. Cade took the opportunity to slip out of the corner and down the aisle. The stallion swung its head over and took a nip at him, but missed. It was a warning. Cade held up his hands. "Easy there boy, Easy now."

"His name is Apple," Jenny said.

"Apple?" Cade didn't move. Apple snorted and stomped a front hoof. "I don't blame you, boy; a name like that would upset me too," Cade said.

Apple bent his head down and charged Jenny. Cade grabbed her and pulled her against him as Apple flew past. The wayward horse continued down to the other end of the barn. He would have held on to her longer, had it not been for her shoving away.

"We have to shut the side door or he can still get out."

Cade was right behind her as they ran down the aisle and hung a right toward another row of stalls.

"We can trap him here and make him go back to his stall."

"Can't take that chance, if he races past us and gets out, we'll never get him back," Jenny said, breathless as she ran down the aisle. Cade grunted and followed, unable to keep up with her. His ribs ached and his leg was as good as a peg on the wall.

Apple charged again. Smacking Cade's shoulder and knocking him into the sawdust. Now that just made him mad. He grunted again, pulling himself up to his feet. He felt a hand take him by the arm. Jenny tugged on him and Cade pulled away from her.

"Watch!" She yanked on his arm again, this time half on his feet. He stumbled forward and pinned her against the wall. Behind him Apple ran bucking and rearing down the aisle.

He could smell her sweet perfume, heady like fresh wild flowers on a warm day. They were hard pressed together, with Jenny's arms trapped against her chest and his hands braced against the wall. He looked down and their eyes met. Her cheeks flushed and the tips of her ears turned a brighter shade of red than her hair.

Cade cleared his throat and stepped back.

In the center aisle, Apple snorted. Cade turned and limped toward the horse. He peered at the stallion. "Had your fun now?"

"What are you doing?" Jenny asked, now standing beside him.

"You want him back in his stall don't you?" Cade asked. He started walking toward Apple, "You go stand by the door and slide it shut once he's in."

Jenny gasped, "Me? What are you going to do?"

Cade snorted. He shook his head. Women! He took one look

at the stallion and grinned. "Don't blame you one bit being locked up. Need to stretch your legs a bit huh?"

Apple didn't pay him any mind. The buckskin stallion ran his teeth over the bars of a stall housing a small pony. A few stalls down, several horses romped in their spaces, anxious from the chaos in the aisle way.

Jenny stood down at the bottom of the aisle clinging to Apple's stall door.

Cade took a deep breath, his ribs in protest, but he wasn't about to let a horse get the best of him. Determined, he walked toward the horse. Apple moved further up the aisle nipping at a bay gelding. The gelding spun around and kicked at the stallion, water splashed from a bucket drenching the stallion's face.

Cade chuckled. Apple whipped his head around and glared at him. "Well, if you wouldn't put your nose where it didn't belong." He got a good laugh out of that. Apple, however, took it as an insult, slightly rearing back.

Cade reached in his pocket. All he had was a piece of peppermint gum. He opened the stick of gum and held it out. The horse murmured low in its throat. He kept one eye on Cade. Apple's nostrils flared taking in the scent of the peppermint. When Cade thought Apple would reach for the gum in his hand he reached out and grabbed the stallion's halter.

Jenny cried out as the stallion lifted Cade off his feet. He tried hard to dig in his heels, but the stallion was determined to shake him off.

He dropped the gum and grabbed onto the halter with both hands. Apple, despite the weight on his head, took off dragging Cade down the aisle. Apple lowered and shook his head. Cade released the halter and laid belly down. Apple snorted above him. Cade felt the stallion's lips twitch across his hair and the hot breath rush down his neck.

He held his breath. He heard the horse snort again and back away from him. Slowly, he turned his head and watched. Apple's muzzle glided across the dirt aisle floor. He didn't move.

Apple turned away, savaging the floor. Jenny took a step forward and Apple's head shot back up. Cade held his hand out to Jenny for her to stay. He pushed himself up to a sitting position. After a moment, Apple ignored them and went back to his scavenger hunt.

Cade pulled himself up.

Apple picked up the discarded piece of gum and chewed on it.

Cade laughed. Apple trotted away from him.

Cade motioned for Jenny to remain silent and stand still. He reached into his pocket again for another piece of gum. Apple sniffed down at the lower corner of the aisle by his stall. Cade walked up beside Jenny, his fingers pressed to his lips. She nodded.

He unwrapped the gum and tossed it inside the stall. Looking back at Jenny he wrinkled his nose.

Jenny shrugged.

Apple spun around, his nose in the air. Another horse whinnied down the way and Jenny said, "Shh!!!"

Apple jumped back, spooked by the sound.

Cade glanced at her and shook his head.

Apple snorted again, this time his nose through the threshold of his stall. Cade put his hand on Jenny's arm. He could feel her trembling hand poised at the stall door and ready to push.

Apple took a step into the stall, his nose rutting through scattered straw and sawdust.

Cade leaned closer, "Wait for it."

Apple took another step, found the gum Cade had tossed in and with his rump just inside the door Jenny shoved the door down the track. Apple whirled around as Cade slipped the latch down and locked the stall door.

"Whoo ...wee!!" He laughed leaning against the door and holding onto his ribs. Sweat poured down over his forehead.

"This isn't funny." Jenny crossed her arms. "Someone could have gotten hurt."

"Well, let's see here. A couple of broken ribs, a bruise here and there. Nope, still in the same condition as when I got here." He grinned at her.

Jenny bit her lip. She glared at him for a long moment. "And the leg? Or did you forget about that all ready?"

Cade pushed away from the wall. "It's kind of hard to forget about something you've been carrying around for half your life."

CHAPTER 13

"I'm sorry," Jenny stammered. "I-I didn't m-mean ..."

"Don't be," Cade interjected, "Sometimes we learn things the hard way. Let's just say it was one of those lessons that you carry around with you the rest of your life." He grasped his hip.

"Let's get you up to the house, we can deal with this guy later," Jenny hooked a thumb toward Apple. Her pulse raced, from Apple's escape and not the man standing near her, she assured herself.

"Seems to me a horse can't let himself out of a stall." Cade inspected the door. "Who was the last one to feed him?"

"I was," Jenny said. "But no one usually opens his stall. His feed is poured in through the bars."

"So how do you clean his stall?"

"Twice a month we put up shoots and run him into the stall across the aisle." Jenny looked at her watch. Josh should be at the house by now with supper. Suddenly she was ravished.

"Twice a month? I thought this place was for rescuing horses from abuse not subjecting them more abuse."

Cade's words struck a chord inside her. Her ire raised and she stood on tippy toe jabbing her finger into his chest. "That's exactly what we do!"

Cade's eyebrow rose.

"We rehabilitate horses and match them with loving owners."

Cade grabbed hold of her finger jabbed into the middle of his chest. "And making horses stomp in their own waste for days on end helps rehabilitate them how?"

Jenny gritted her teeth. She jerked her finger from his grasp. "Apple's a special case."

"Really? Perhaps you should tell me more on our way to supper," he said, hearing her stomach rumble.

Jenny clasped her stomach and felt the heat rush to her cheeks.

Cade gave her arm a little nudge, "Come on, I'll walk you to the house and you can tell me all about him."

Jenny glanced up at him. Cade was about a foot taller. She sighed. How could a man like Cade Sheridan understand? Then again, she didn't know much about him. Was he even a Christian? Did it even matter?

Deep down, she knew it did.

"As I've told you his name is Apple. He only responds to human contact for long enough to swipe an apple from you hand. He came here last spring, wild and unpredictable."

"Not much has changed, I see."

Jenny gave him a look and proceeded as they walked toward the stable doors. "He doesn't lead."

"No kidding." Cade flexed his arm.

"Do you want to know this or not?" Jenny asked, tugging on the stable doors. Cade reached over and helped her push.

"We tried letting him out into the outdoor arena once, but he got loose. We were able to catch him a few days later. Thankfully, he'd run into one of pastures with a few mares. "

"Sounds like he had his only little herd going. How old is he?"

Jenny walked out into the fading afternoon. A glowing orange ball hung low in the sky and clouds stretched across the horizon, evaporating for the night.

"Michael thinks he's under five, but can't tell for sure without being able to look at his teeth."

"And Michael is Sarah's husband?" Cade asked.

Jenny nodded. "Michael's the veterinarian and Sarah's the horse trainer."

"And you?"

"I manage the clinic, and help out here at the stables," Jenny said.

"It seems to me you all have your hands full."

By now Jenny had her hand on the front door knob. She turned and looked up at him over her shoulder. "We manage."

"Perhaps I can give you all a hand while I'm here. After all, you've given me a place to stay and three square meals a day since I've been here."

"I'm sure the last thing the doctor ordered when I picked you up at the hospital was to hurt yourself again by trying to handle horses that have behavior issues."

Cade stepped in her way of opening the door. "I've been around horses since the day I could walk. I've rode and worked with just about every kind of horse you can find. I've done my time bustin' broncs, even after one tried busting me." He tapped his leg.

"Oh ..." She looked at his hip and looked up at his face. Chiseled lines, like those on the palm of a hand, told his story. She wanted to reach up and touch his face, trace those furrowed lines across his forehead and down the side of his cheek.

He stepped out the way and opened the door for Jenny. He motioned for her to go first. She found everyone in the kitchen. Michael stood leaning against the kitchen counter with a piece of dripping cheese pizza. Sarah and Ethan sat side by side at the table with Ellie, Ethan's Beagle dog, begging at his feet. She glanced around the corner and frowned. "Where's Josh?"

"Since when does Josh stick around when there's an auction somewhere?" Sarah said, "Oh hello Mr. Sheridan. Please have a seat and join us. Sorry I don't have a home cooked meal to offer you tonight."

"But we've got pizza." Ethan held up his slice to show Cade. Elle barked beneath the table.

"Don't need to make a fuss over me, Mrs. Wolfe, pizza is just fine," Cade said.

"As I've said before, just call me 'Sarah'."

Jenny smiled. She loved seeing Sarah so happy. They'd never had the time to be like other best friends, imagining weddings and babies together. Sarah had been well on her way to being a mother when they declared best friend status after that first summer they met.

She missed part of the conversation, but watched Cade shake Michael's hand. She reached around the men and grabbed two plates. Placing a slice on for herself and two on for Cade, she offered him a plate.

Cade leaned against the counter by Michael, an open pizza box between them and another on the table. Jenny grabbed drinks from the refrigerator and sat beside Sarah. They hung out in the kitchen for the evening, talking horses and motorcycles.

Tense at first, Cade soon relaxed and laughed along with them. How easy he seemed to fit in amongst them. She watched him scoop up another slice of pizza and converse with Michael.

Sarah soon tapped her on the shoulder, and they left the males to the kitchen and retreated outside to the swing.

Jenny sat and held up her feet for Sarah to rock the swing. Out in the yard, the lush greens of summer wilted from the late July heat. An orange hue rested over the stables, and out in the far pastures horses grazed with their tails swaying in the gentle breeze.

"Thank you for taking care of that paperwork here at the barn and tending to the horses," Sarah said. "I was getting ready to send Michael out to help before you came in with Cade."

"Apple got loose in the barn. Cade helped me put him back," Sarah would have found out one way or another.

"Got out? How did he get out?" Sarah stopped rocking.

Jenny sighed, "It doesn't matter. He didn't do any harm. Cade fell and got dragged a few feet."

"Jenny!"

Jenny took Sarah by the arm. "It's okay, really. Don't get up."

Sarah leaned back into the rocker, her face a mesh of worry lines and dark circles. "Okay? Earth to Jenny! Cade got dragged by a horse!"

"It's not like he hasn't ever been drug before. Besides, he's fine. Apple's fine. All is well."

Everything didn't feel well. Sarah frowned and placed her hand on her heart. "Jenny … I know Brad hurt you, but this …"

"What?" She didn't know why, but Jenny felt hot tears in her eyes. She was done crying. Done dating, and done letting men break her heart. *Thanks God, but no thanks. If you can't bring a guy into my life that's a keeper, then don't bring him at all.*

"You've smashed a motorcycle, almost killed a man … more than once, and what about Apple? We could have lost him."

"I didn't almost kill Cade." Jenny said, crossing her arm.

Sarah looked at her.

"Okay, maybe once. Getting dragged by Apple wasn't my fault. It wasn't like I told him to grab the halter."

"No," Sarah sighed, "It's my fault. I should have done something with Apple a long time ago."

"You did have to go get married, didn't you," Jenny glanced at Sarah.

A slow smile spread across Sarah's face. "What kind of faithful servant would I be not to follow the plan the Lord has for me?"

"I remember a time when you didn't think that way."

Sarah shifted on the swing and looked at Jenny, "Only because someone I knew needed to give me a little boost. Maybe you do too."

"I don't need a boost, I need," Jenny paused. She shrugged, "It doesn't matter what I need. Brad is gone, Cade will be leaving soon, and things will be back to the way they were before."

"Not the way they were before. I'm having a baby remember?"

How could she forget? They weren't sixteen anymore, but

back then it seemed so much simpler. She was always there for Sarah, and now Sarah had Michael.

Josh was off and running, he didn't even show up for Sunday dinner hardly anymore. And with Brad gone? *Oh Lord, what plans do you have for me?*

"Before it snows, I'm sure."

Sarah rubbed her protruding stomach, "Which means another winter for Apple to stand unattended."

"At least he's being fed and taken care of," Jenny said.

"He hasn't really calmed down since he's come here, and I haven't had the time to devote to him that he needs."

"I can help."

"You're stretched between the clinic and the rescue as it is," Sarah said.

"Then we'll find someone," jenny said.

Sarah nodded. "I'll speak to Michael, but not tonight. Tonight, I'm going to bed, this baby is starting to get heavier to carry around these days."

They both looked up as the front door opened.

Cade stepped out on the porch. Sarah struggled to stand up and both Jenny and Cade reached for her at the same time. She took Cade's offered hand.

"I didn't mean to interrupt," Cade said.

"You didn't," Sarah assured him, "I was just on my way into the house."

Jenny stood with Sarah. She lingered by the swing, watching Cade open the door and murmured good night to Sarah. His deep voice was like a plucked bass string vibrating in the humid evening air.

Once Sarah was inside the house, Jenny said goodnight and headed off the porch.

"Wait," said Cade, "I'll walk you home."

"No need," she didn't know why but she felt as if she needed to escape him. Goosebumps ran up her arms, despite her long sleeves, and she shivered in the evening air.

"Then may I just join you on your walk? It's not like we're not going in the same direction."

Michael must have told him that she lived in his old apartment above the clinic. She'd moved in after Sarah and Michael tied the knot. She shrugged, trying to pretend it didn't matter, but somehow it did.

Cade fell into step beside her and they walked down the lane. He would be gone soon. What did she care? He'd be gone in less time than bringing in a crop and she had no intentions of becoming the harvest.

Let both grow together until the harvest, and at the harvest I will tell the reapers gather the weeds first and bind them in bundles to be burned, but gather the wheat for in my barn.

This quote from Matthew spoke to her from her heart. She walked faster. Despite his limp, Cade adjusted his stride and maintained his place beside her. Ordinarily, she would have gazed up at the stars, wonder, and say a little wish. As silly as it was, she knew no wish could give her what her heart desired; only God and acceptance would heal the heart of Brad's deception.

As they reached the bridge, sounds of the waters made a sweet melody along with the crickets singing at their approach.

"You can go on from here, I'll be fine." Truth was, she'd wanted this time to herself. The walk would have given her time to think, pray, and exhaust the pent up frustrations she'd carried.

There was so much to do, and even more so with Sarah being pregnant. Oh, Sarah protested plenty when Jenny shoved her in the office and gave her the paper work to do while she, Josh, and Ethan took care of the barn.

What would they do when Sarah was so pregnant she couldn't help at all? OR after the baby came, how would she manage to balance mothering two and caring for the horses?

Jenny looked over at Cade. He was frowning, his brow wrinkled, and his arm wrapped around his ribs.

What if Sarah was right?

Cade could have been killed.

A trickle of sweat glinted on his brown in the twilight. "You should go back to the cottage and lie down."

"As soon as I see you to your apartment," Cade gritted his teeth.

Jenny stopped, turned, and placed her hands on her hips. She opened her mouth, about to give Cade a piece of her mind and halted. Cade stood taking deep breaths through his nose and exhaling through his mouth.

"You're hurting."

"Nothing a few aspirin won't cure later." He winced as he tried to take her arm and walk her down the lane.

Jenny didn't move. His grip on her arm was gentle, but rather than guiding her, he clung to her for support.

His hair line grew damp and his face turned white.

"Whoa now, you're not going to pass out on me are you?" Jenny held onto him.

Cade shook his head. He focused on her, staring into her eyes. Pain filling his expression. Her heart thumped in her chest.

"You need to sit down."

Cade shook his head again, although he bent forward at the same time.

"I'll go get Sarah's car. Just stay here," she said, pushing him back against the side of the bridge. Cade stepped back and slid down the wall. "Kind of pushy, aren't you?"

"Only when necessary."

CHAPTER 14

"I didn't expect to see you this morning. How are you feeling?" Sarah asked.

Cade placed a protective hand over his ribs. He didn't like to admit when he was down. He didn't like being in anyone's debt. Maybe he should call it even between him and Jenny. After all, when he first met her, she'd nearly gotten him killed, and then last night she'd saved him.

The emergency room doctor confirmed that Apple had caused additional stress on his cracked ribs and prolonged his healing time.

"A might sore, but I'll manage. And you?"

Sarah laughed, "Growing larger every day." She patted her pregnant belly. "If you're looking for Jenny, she's over at the clinic."

"Ah yes, well I wasn't really looking for Jenny. Not really. I was on my way to visit Apple when I saw you in here. I hope you don't mind if I have a man to man talk with the dominant resident of the stables."

Sarah leaned forward on her elbows. It appeared awkward stretching her arms over her belly to touch the desk. It couldn't have been comfortable.

"You still want to see him after what he did to you?"

"I'd like to spend some time with him. I've broken a few hors-es in my time and trained a few here and there."

"Really?" Sarah sat up, taking a sudden interest in what he said. "Are you thinking you'd like to adopt Apple then?"

Truth was, the thought had never crossed his mind. "And hitch him to the back of my motorcycle?"

"Or ride him off into the sunset on four legs rather than two?"

Cade had to admit that Sarah's wit was refreshing compared to Jenny's brisk replies. "I prefer a little more horse power when I'm riding than even a stallion like Apple can provide."

Funny, he didn't even miss his motorcycle or the fact that he wasn't able to go anywhere except the stables, clinic, and the old stone farmhouse for the past week.

"I'll admit that I could use an extra hand around here, but are you sure you're feeling up to it? I mean according to Jenny your ribs were re-fractured and you're to take it easy while they heal."

"If you don't mind me saying so, there's no such thing as easy. Life is rough and hard and we've got to cut our paths and shape our future if we plan on going anywhere."

Sarah leaned back in her chair. She crossed her arms over her big belly. "I'm a curious sort of person, Cade. I know you're an ex rodeo cowboy. But what I don't know is why you'd want to train a horse like Apple if you have no intentions of making him your own?"

This wasn't fifth grade math, and he didn't like having to ex-plain himself. He rubbed his side and looked at Sarah. Her brown hair hung in a long ponytail down her back and her gaze weary like someone who hadn't slept in days. He didn't think she would deny him his request no matter what he had to say to her. How-ever, he had no intentions of lying to her either.

"I just want to see Apple go to a good home, and if teaching him a little horse etiquette will accomplish that, then I'm willing to be dragged to the moon in back to make it possible."

Sarah's eyebrows shot up.

"Besides it will give me something to do around here other than viewing the scenery."

Sarah reached over at the shrill of the phone. Cade rubbed his side and listened to Sarah speak. A moment later, she hung up and looked at him. "I'm afraid we'll have to put this conversation on hold. I need to find Josh to pick up a horse."

"I take it you're going after a rescue?"

"Yeah, we've been expecting it for some time, but the owner wasn't cooperating until now. His wife passed on a few months ago, the horse belonged to his wife." Sarah glanced down and tapped her fingers on the desk. "Have you seen Josh?"

"Can't say I have, he wasn't in the cottage this morning."

Sarah frowned. "Maybe he's over at the clinic, I'll call Jenny."

Cade left Sarah to her phone call and headed out of the office. He looked down the aisle. Several horses munched on their hay while other stalls appeared empty with their stall doors slid open.

He limped toward Apple's stall.

"Apparently, Josh never came home and Jenny can't leave the clinic with Michael gone on a farm visit. It looks like I'm going to have to do it myself," Sarah said, waddling out into the stable aisle. "I hate to leave. Roger will be coming by this morning with our order from the feed mill."

Cade shook his head. He took one glance down the aisle toward Apple's stall and glanced back over his shoulder at Sarah. She had on an oversized flannel shirt with the sleeves rolled up and her rounded belly protruding out. He turned and held out his hand. "Give me a set of keys and the address, I'll go."

"That's very kind of you ..."

Cade sighed, "But what? I'm a guest?"

"We already owe you so much," Sarah said, "The rescue is ..."

Again he didn't give her a chance to finish, "Donations and volunteers. I'm volunteering. You said it yourself, Josh is M.I.A., Jenny can't leave the clinic while Michael's gone, and Michael can't while he's out on a call. No offense Mrs. Wolfe, feed delivery or not you're in no condition to load up a horse."

Sarah put her hands on her lips, "I'm pregnant, not disabled."

"One bump, nudge, or slam from an unruly horse could put that baby and you both in danger." He swallowed hard. A picture of a blonde haired woman floated across his mind and he pushed the picture away. He didn't want to see her again, least of all now.

"You sound like Michael and Jenny."

"They just want what's best for you," Cade said. "If I didn't want to help, I wouldn't offer."

"Are you always this blunt with others, Mr. Sheridan?"

"My Momma always said I was a little too honest, but that is what she admired the most about me."

"She sounds like a smart lady." A faraway look glazed Sarah's eyes. He recognized that look, understood the grief that caused her eyes to go watery, and could appreciate the grief that crept into her face disguised as frown lines.

"I'm glad to hear that, I didn't think I understood right when Jenny told us you didn't have any family."

"My mother lives in Texas on the ranch she and my father inherited from his father, or at least the last time I saw her."

"How long was that?"

"About ten years." His gut twisted. It still made his throat go raw.

Her sorrow-filled expression deepened. "I lost my parents when I was sixteen. There isn't a day that goes by that I don't miss them. Gram, I suppose in her own way, did her best to look after me and Ethan, but now she's gone too. Family is a precious thing; if I've learned anything it is hold close to those who love you."

Sarah's words choked him. He had known for some time that he needed to go home. Wasn't that where he was going before Silver Wind's trailer pushed him off course?

His chest clogged and as he cleared his throat, Sara said. "I'll write down that address for you. You'll find the keys in the glove box of the truck along with a GPS."

A little while later, Cade stood inspecting the hitch of the trailer to the truck. There were several cars parked in the lot at the clinic. Curious as he was to see inside Silver Wind's Equine Clinic, he needed to pick up that horse for Sarah.

He gave the safety chains one last jiggle when he heard, "What are you doing?"

He turned and came face to face with Jenny. Her hair was held back by two little black clips and her cheeks were pink like the soft hue of a morning sunrise. Her green eyes glared at him.

"Just checking the hitch, don't want it coming loose again do we?" He wiped his hands down his torn jeans and stepped around her.

Her lips pursed out. "You didn't come here to check the hitch."

"Nothing ever slips past you does it?" he asked.

"What are you up to? If you need a ride somewhere I can take you later in my car."

Cade leaned back against the truck. She was a vision all right and not the angelic kind either. She reminded him of a rogue pirate in her black knee high boots and fitted blouse. All she needed was a tattoo to finish the pirate look, but he didn't imagine Jenny would ever mar her perfect skin with something like a tattoo. Not the way his ex-wife Crystal had.

He shook his head. It was the second time since coming here that Crystal crossed his mind. He needed to get a ride and get out of this place before the haunted memories of his past resurfaced.

"Afraid I won't come back?"

She scowled. "I was trying to be nice."

Cade turned away and opened the door. "I'd love to stand around and chit chat like you women do, but I've got to get going. I'll catch you on the way back, pick up some lunch, and you can be 'nice' later."

Jenny grabbed the door. "For your information, I have a lunch date, and you're not taking this truck and trailer anywhere."

Cade gritted his teeth. The woman was more irritating than a pebble in his shoe. He took her by the wrist and she gasped. "You don't ever listen to anything anyone tells you do you? Well, let me tell you that I'm taking this truck and trailer and picking up a horse for Sarah. Lunch or no lunch."

Jenny tipped her face up and stared at him. "Then I'm going with you. *Lunch or no lunch.*"

"What about your date?" Cade asked.

"The ladies in my Bible study will understand, this is rescue business."

"And the clinic?"

"Will be fine until we get back, Doc wouldn't mind and I'll handle the paper work when we return."

"Go back to your clinic, I can handle picking up a horse on my own," Cade said.

"We who are strong have an obligation to bear with the failings of the weak, and not to please ourselves."

"Like to quote scripture, do you? Try this one: 'Do not withhold good from whom it is due, when it is in your power to do it'."

Jenny arched an eyebrow, "Well. Well."

All those years of memorizing bible verses in Sunday school finally paid off. He would have paid the price of two gold buckles for a picture to recapture the look on Jenny's face. He knew it wasn't nice, but a small pressure released in his chest and eased his lungs. "I may be a drifter, but I'm no heathen."

Her jaw dropped and he got in the truck.

CHAPTER 15

He chuckled from inside the cab watching Jenny march around to the other side of the truck. She yanked open the door and hopped in beside him. She crossed her arm and glared at him. He reached across her lap, opened the glove box and pulled out the keys. Jenny pushed back into the seat while he set up the GPS on the dash and closed the glove box.

He stuck the key in the engine and waited.

She continued to glare at him, "Are we going or what?"

"Seat belt?"

She looked down at her lap, then grabbed her seat belt and pulled it across her lap. Her arms crossed, she said, "Ready now?"

He started up the engine.

"You'll need to put the lights on there," she pointed to the switch on the dash, "And make sure ..."

He held up a hand, "I got it, thanks."

She pouted. Cute as it was, it irritated him. She turned her attention to watching the trailer turn behind them as he backed out of the lot and headed for the road.

She reached over and turned on the music from the truck stereo. Cade reached over and switched it off. She scowled at him, but didn't say a word the rest of the ride from Silver Wind to the rescue horse's location.

Twenty minutes later, they turned down the drive to a small ranch, and parked in front of a small stable, Jenny hopped out of the truck before Cade could shut off the engine. Determination set on her face, she strode over to the broken hinged door.

Cade got out. He spied an old man stepping down off his porch.

Jenny jerked the door and Cade grabbed it. "Just hold up there Nellie."

"Nellie?"

"Yeah. Don't tell me you've never heard the expression."

"Are you referring that I'm an old nag?"

He suppressed a grin and shrugged.

"We've got to get in there, who knows what shape that horse is in," Jenny said.

"The owner is on his way," Cade said. They both watched as an old man hobbled toward them. The porch roof of the house leaned to the left corner. Tall grass and brittle weeds spread as far as the eye could see.

"Let me handle this," Jenny headed toward the man. The old man came up short as Jenny laid into him, "Sir, I'm with Silver Wind Equine Rescue and we're here to take possession of the poor animal you have in that barn." She pointed to the broken door.

"I don't know about calling Ole Sheldon poor, a little neglected since the missus went, but poor he isn't."

"Mind if we go inside?" Cade asked.

"Suit yourself, watch the door though, the hinge broke off the roller last week and haven't been able to get it fixed." The old man walked around Jenny and lent Cade a hand in lifting the stable door and sliding it back. Cade didn't imagine the old man had much success in opening and closing the door on his own. The place, like its owner, was aged and needing some repairs.

Jenny shoved her way between them and entered the dim light stables. A soft knicker came from the first stall on the right.

Immediately, she turned. Cade stepped in behind her followed by the old man.

Over the stall door the head of a large Belgian gelding greeting them.

"That there be Sheldon," the old man said.

"Why he doesn't look abused at all," Jenny patted Sheldon on the side of his cheek. She ran her hand down his neck and peeked into his stall.

"I would hope not," said the old man, his voice gruff. "Took right good care of him, my Mae did. Best plow horse we ever did have. Tilled up the garden ever spring and Mae would hitch him to the Surry on Sundays and take the grandkids for a ride."

"So you're surrendering him?"

Sheldon gave Jenny a shove forward and Cade caught her before she fell on her face.

"Getting harder to get around these days. Mae won't be making anymore gardens or taking any more Sunday rides, but Sheldon here, he's still got spunk in him."

Jenny walked over to the old man, "Your wife was Mae Zimmerman."

The old man nodded, pulled out his hankie and blew his nose. "You knew my wife?"

Jenny placed her hand on the old man's arm, "I wish I had, but your daughter Kristen attends our bible study when she can. We all prayed with her when your wife had grown so ill."

Mr. Zimmerman dabbed the tears from his weary eyes. Even Cade felt his own throat tightening. He reached up by the stall and grabbed the lead rope. Snapping it onto Sheldon's halter, the horse murmured and pressed his muzzle to Cade's shirt pocket.

"He's lookin' for a carrot." Mr. Zimmerman reached in his pocket, "Got one left just for today."

Jenny took the carrot from Mr. Zimmerman and fed it to Sheldon. Satisfied with his snack, Sheldon nodded his head. Cade unlatched the stall door and led the large work horse out of the stable.

Jenny rushed up to the trailer and opened the doors. As Cade loaded the horse, he heard Jenny speaking with Mr. Zimmerman. Sheldon stepped right up onto the trailer, the matted floor beneath him shook.

Cade had no problems leading the old horse to the front and tying him. He patted Sheldon on the neck and walked back down off the trailer.

He shut the back door and latched it, keeping an eye on Jenny. She hugged the tearful old man and said, "We'll see he gets the best home, and you're welcome to come visit him in the meantime."

Mr. Zimmerman shook his head. "I'll be moving on soon. My son and his family in Virginia have asked me to come live with them. Got three grandkids down there you know, Beth's gonna have another one and these ole knees still got some bouncin' in them."

"What are you going to do with this place?"

Cade gazed out over the property. In its own little way, it reminded him of the small ranch back home in Texas. His heart ached with the sudden loss.

"Imagine I'll sell it. Got to fix it up a little first. Hate to leave the place, you know. Built that barn myself. My, that was the day, we weren't married six days and we bought this place. The whole town came and we had ourselves one big party inside when it was done."

"That must have been some party," Cade said.

"That it was, that is was …. Well, I suppose you two need to be off, just me and Hester now."

It was then they noticed the chicken clucking around the front yard.

"I'll walk you back to your porch, Mr. Zimmerman. Someone will be back out soon for you to sign the official surrender papers. You have ten days to reclaim him if you change your mind."

CHAPTER 16

Jenny unlocked the door and walked through the clinic, stopping in each room to flick on the lights. She checked the coffee pot in the break room, percolating as scheduled, and satisfied everything was in its place, she headed to her desk.

A little red light blinked on the answering machine. She pressed the button for the recorder to play back the messages received from last evening before she sat in her chair and flipped open her laptop. She grabbed a pen, poised to write down information from the callers while watching for the software to boot up on the computer screen.

Mr. Drutmyer's horse was lame and needed Michael to stop by on his next farm visit. Douglas McDonald had a cow sick. Jenny sighed and made a note to call them when she paused at the recognition of Brad's voice next in the record.

"Hey Jen. I know you're mad at me, probably why you won't answer your phone. If it makes any difference I haven't seen my wife in years, we just stay married for the kids ...."

Jenny rolled her eyes. She didn't want to hear anything more he had to say, but she couldn't quite bring herself to reach over and hit the skip or erase button. Her heart held fast in her chest, like a cube of water turning to ice.

"Anyway, I'm coming back through town in a week or two, thought maybe we could see each other. Weren't you the one that always believed in second chances and all?"

And then the recorder cut off his voice with a loud beep and announced there were no more messages.

Jenny took a deep rattled breath. She pressed her hand to her heart, squeezing her eyes shut, and bit down on her lip. She prayed because it was the only thing she knew that would bring distraction enough to keep her heart from aching.

"He's a married man," she whispered. "Thou shall not commit adultery."

Overhead, the bell jingled as the front door rattled.

Jenny opened her eyes. "I'm coming." She jumped out of the chair and rushed across the clinic's waiting area.

Doc Miller scowled at her from the other side of the glass door. Fumbling, she managed to turn the lock and pull the door open. Doc Miller grunted. "A little late aren't you, Girly?"

"It wouldn't hurt for you to spare me some mercy some time, "Jenny told him.

Doc Miller waved his hand as he walked inside the clinic, "Phooey. Next you'll be tellin' me that your boyfriend dumped you and you're just so heartbroken that you forgot to unlock the door."

Jenny released the door, dumbfounded.

Doc Miller shook a finger at her, "I might be old, but I'm not deaf. Ain't no man around that could keep up with a spirited lass like you."

Jenny laughed, it eased the hard lump that was her heart and made it soften. She smiled, "If only you were forty years younger."

"I'd still be a married man," he said, matter of fact.

Jenny followed him back to her desk. "All the good ones usually are."

Doc Miller grabbed a lab coat from a peg near the hallway and chuckled. "You just wait, Girly, the good Lord's got something special in store for you.

Jenny picked up a folder on the corner of her desk. "Your first appointment is due in fifteen minutes."

"Straight to the point. That's what I like about you."

"You're married, remember?" Jenny said, putting a hand on her hip.

Doc Miller chuckled. "And don't you forget it."

They both turned at the sound of the bell jingle. She expected to see Doc Miller's first appointment stepping through the door, but when she looked up, Mr. Carr strolled through the door with a stack of packages in his arms.

He smiled at her and she smiled in return. The handsome young mailman unloaded his packages on the corner of his desk.

"This one requires a signature," he told her.

As she signed for the package she spied the envelope on the top of the stack. It was addressed to Cade.

"You have a good day now," he said. Jenny waved and Doc Miller turned and walked down the hall away from her.

Mr. Carr held open the door and a tall thin woman walked inside the clinic with a tall sleek Doberman at her side.

Jenny picked up the envelope, staring at Cade's name.

In the meantime, Jenny hadn't heard the bell, and a woman walked up and signed a sheet at the end of Jenny's desk before she took a seat. How did anyone know that Cade was here? She realized then it was Cade's check from the insurance company. Since she had no other information to give them, she'd given them the clinic's address. How soon would it take Cade to find a new motorcycle and hightail it out of Silver Wind?

She should be happy, but somehow the thought caused a confliction of emotion. One she'd feel for a broken winged bird or kid losing an ice cream. She shook her head. No, it didn't feel like that at all. It just plain made her sad and she didn't know why.

This is what she wanted—to help Cade and move on—wasn't it?

"Seems to me you can sit around staring at checks on your

own time. Don't seem to have any patients in any of the rooms down the hall, now do I?"

Warmth spread up her neck and over her cheeks. She dropped the letter and snatched up a folder. "Getting to it right now," she said.

Doc Miller shook his baldhead.

Michael returned later in the afternoon. She carried a package out to the clinic. She spotted Michael's truck parked by the open doors. He opened and shut the small compartments of the truck's bed.

"I've got those meds you ordered last week, where do you want them?"

"Here, I'll take them," Michael said.

Jenny held them out. "Did you get the add-ons to your schedule this morning?" They'd started a new system and Jenny could update Michael's schedule from her laptop right into his notebook computer while he was on the road.

"Yeah, Mr. Drutmyer is going to be bringing his horse this evening for x-rays. Not much I can do for McDonald's cow."

"Well, we all do what we can, right?"

Michael closed up the last compartment. "Miller still here?"

"No, he left about an hour ago. Mrs. Miller had stew on the table waiting for him." Jenny fell into step beside Michael and he reached for the package in her arms. "I was hoping he would take a look at some results from the lab on the Mullin's race horse."

Jenny couldn't ever get over how much Sarah's son Ethan looked more and more like his father, Michael, each day. And to think that once upon a time not so long ago, Michael didn't have a clue that the boy belonged to him.

"Everything all right?"

"Not sure, but we won't worry about it until Doc can confirm the results with me."

"Oh," Jenny said.

"I'll need you to add Apple to the schedule next week. Sarah wants him gelded."

"If that would do him any good," Jenny said.

"Take down his temperament a bit, and with Cade working with him, we should have him in a new home in no time."

"Cade?" Jenny stepped into the clinic's medical storage room. Michael sat down the box and pulled out its contents.

"Nice of him to offer. Sarah couldn't have done much, pregnant as she is and even after the baby comes we've been thinking of adding someone around here to help train the horses."

A small, slow, burning spread through the pit of her stomach. "But we don't need anybody else, were managing just fine. Besides we don't have the money to pay a trainer at the rescue."

Michael sat the last of the liquid medicines into a glass door fridge. "Are you going to train the horses? Listen Jenny, I appreciate you managing the clinic the way you do, but face it. With you here, Josh always on the run hauling, and with Sarah soon to have two boys under her feet, Sarah won't be able to manage the rescue and train the horses."

Jenny opened her mouth to object. Did Michael know what he was saying? She could do it. She could do all of it if she had to. Hadn't she always been there for Sarah before when Ethan was born and they graduated from high school? Even when Jenny went off to college, she returned to help Sarah.

Michael put his hand on her shoulder, "We're not worried about the money. The insurance deductible set us back a little for your accident, but God will provide, we have no doubt that things will work out for the best where the rescue is concerned."

Jenny crossed her arms. "That's why we're in this together. A team."

"That's why we need one more member of the team to help us. And now we've got Cade."

"Cade's not a member of our team."

Michael walked past her, saying as he left, "You never know, maybe your running into Cade was a blessing. He can train horses, after all."

She turned and scowled at Michael's retreating back. Isn't that what she'd said to Sarah when Michael had moved in next door to Silver Wind and started building this clinic? Maybe Cade coming here was in God's plan for Silver Wind, but not in Jenny's.

No, this wasn't the plan. She brought Cade here so she could help him and move on. How could she do that if he stayed? Is *this your plan, God? If this is your plan to bring Cade here, then what plans do you have for me?*

Thoughts of Cade Sheridan stirred something inside her.

Love thy neighbor ...

It was what she'd always been taught, but she didn't know if she could.

CHAPTER 17

By the next Saturday afternoon, a regular stream of people was floating through the rescue barn. Sarah worked in the office, taking applications and talking to folks interested in adopting one of the rescue horses.

Cl There were new faces and some coming back who weren't sure from the first time, that adopting a rescue horse was right for them. Outside, ponies ran in the corral and Josh hung by the fence talking to a pretty blonde haired woman. No doubt he was asking for her phone number for more than a contact for one of the horses, Jenny thought, as she entered the barn.

Most of the stalls were clean with nameplates and adoption information posted on the stall doors. Towards the back, away from the rest of the people, Jenny spotted a lonely cowboy. He tipped his hat in greeting as she approached.

"Can I help you?"

He grinned, revealing a white-toothy grin. "Nice looking stallion you've got here."

Jenny looked through the bars of the stall doors. Looking back at the man she said, "He's not yet available for adoption."

"Shame," the man said, "He's one of the best horses I've seen here today. You sure you won't adopt him out?"

Jenny tugged on the hem of her t-shirt with the Silver Wind Equine Rescue logo. "We only adopt out horses that we know are suitable for their new owners. Apple still needs trained."

"Training him wouldn't be a problem. I'd actually quite enjoy working with horses like him."

"I have no doubt," Jenny said.

"Call me Bailey, and you are?"

"Jenny." Her cheeks grew hot as he took her hand and lifted it to his lips. Down the barn aisle, she spotted Cade limping toward them. She pulled her hand away from Bailey and put it behind her back.

"Short for Jennifer, right?"

"No. It's just Jenny."

Inside the stall, Apple turned away from them, his ears laid back and his one leg poised as if he would kick at the slightest movement.

"Well, Just Jenny, I bet this stallion is a real handful for you folks."

"Apple just needs some TLC and a whole lot of patience. He'll come around. You never know, maybe this time next year, he'll be adoptable."

Bailey tipped his hat up and scratched his head. "That's a mighty long time to make a horse wait. Is that your trainer up there, the pregnant gal?"

Jenny tilted her head. She kept one eye on Cade as he got closer and one eye on Bailey. "Yes, that's Sarah. She founded Silver Wind Equine Rescue."

"Be a long time before she'll have the opportunity to train this animal, having a baby and running the rescue and all …"

"I wouldn't be so sure."

They both turned and looked at Cade.

"Well if it isn't Cade Sheridan. I haven't seen you since you took the championship buckle over in Dover. What's that been now?"

"Not nearly long enough." Cade's jaw twitched.

"You two know each other?"

"What are you doing here, Bailey?" Cade asked, ignoring Jenny's question.

"I don't think that's any of your business now, is it?"

"Anything that has to do with this place is my business," Cade said.

"I heard you were taking on some mean horses since leaving the circuit. Well, they won't have to waste their funds on this one, I plan to take him back with me," Bailey hooked his thumbs in his belt loops.

"As I said before, Apple's not adoptable," Jenny said.

"You won't find anything you're looking for here, Bailey." Cade stepped closer behind Jenny. Her short spikes of hair were mere inches from his neck.

Bailey's eyes narrowed, but then his lips split open into a big grin. "I don't know about that. Seems to me I found a prize without even having to look." Dillon winked at Jenny.

Her cheeks flushed pink, she opened her mouth to say something, but she felt Cade's hand rest on her shoulder. "You're wasting your time here."

"That depends on whether Jenny's available for dinner tonight," Bailey looked right at Jenny. She'd never been so tongue tied in her life as she was now. The answer stuck at the inside of her lips, but before she could reply, Cade tugged her closer and asked, "I think you've got some Bible study meeting going on tonight, don't you?"

Jenny frowned. "That's not till Wednesday."

"I think you need to check your calendar again," Cade squeezed her shoulder tighter.

"Why don't I give you my card and you can give me a call when you're available." Bailey reached into his shirt pocket and handed her a business card.

"I'm sure you will," Cade said, as Bailey walked away.

Jenny waited until Bailey was far enough away before yanking his arm off her. Cade winced. "Just who do you think you are?"

she asked.

"You'd be wise to stay clear of guys like Bailey, they're nothing but trouble."

"Why? Because you know him or because he's married?" Jenny asked.

Cade stared at her a long moment. She had that chin of hers tilted again and her arms crossed. Those vibrant green eyes of hers stared so sharply at him that if he weren't too careful, he just might find them piercing into his heart.

"Men like Bill Bailey don't marry." With that, he limped away. He'd had enough of the subject of Bailey. Hazy images of broken down horses and smoky bar rooms turned his gut sour and made his head spin.

Thankfully, Jenny didn't press him or follow him outside the barn, Cade leaned against the corral. He spotted Josh at the far corner picking up a boy and putting him into the saddle atop a pony.

Josh, like his sister, had red hair, but the comparison stopped there. He didn't see too much of the guy he shared a house with these past few days. He'd heard the door open and shut at night and late night phone calls coming from Josh's cell phone. Once he'd been tempted to answer it, then Josh had walked out, picked up the phone, then hung it up again.

Something didn't smell right with Jenny's brother, and it wasn't the dirty laundry lying on the couch, either.

"Hey, Cade,"

Cade looked down at Sarah and Michael's boy, Ethan. He was about seven and had that small yipping Beagle at his side.

"Are you going to adopt a pony? Cause that one right there that they're riding is mine," Ethan said. "I just let them borrow Pudge for rides."

"That's a mighty fine looking pony, but I'm afraid my horse days are over."

Ethan tilted his head to the side and looked up at Cade. "Is that because Aunt Jenny broke your bike?"

Cade smiled. He liked this kid, straight to the point. From the boy's dark raven hair and sharp blue eyes, this kid was intelligent. Michael and Sarah Wolfe were nice folks, but Cade hadn't wanted to impose upon them any more than just having a place to sleep while he waited for the insurance check.

Back in the day, he would have thought it his right. After all, as Ethan said, Jenny was responsible for "breaking" his motorcycle. Only there were too many pieces to put it together again.

"Motorcycles can be fixed or replaced," Cade said. "But not people."

"That's why you're here, so you can get better." He grinned up at Cade. "Then you can ride Pudge, he's really friendly."

Cade mussed Ethan's hair, "I think I'm a little too big for ponies, but thanks for the offer."

"We've got other horses. You could always take one home with you. Just not Bonnie, she belongs to my mom. And Clyde is dad's horse. He's kind of temperamental," Ethan said.

Cade almost wanted to say, "Like your Aunt Jenny." He limped over closer to the end of the corral to take a better look at Ethan's pony.

"Did that happen when you fell off your bike?" Ethan followed Cade.

Cade shook his head. It had been a long time since he'd been around kids this age. He imaged they were a curious lot. No harm in being curious, he leaned his elbows on the top rail of the corral and looked in at the pony.

"Been limping like this since I was sixteen. Let's just say my first lesson in riding horses was a rough one."

Ethan's eyes grew large, "Is that why you don't ride anymore?"

Cade sighed and looked over at the boy, "There hasn't been a horse that's gotten the best of me since, Kid. Now women, however, are a whole different story."

Ethan made a face, and Cade knew he'd confused the boy. He hunched down the best he could and looked Ethan in the eye. "Sometimes it takes owning up to our own faults to make things right in your life. It's a part of growing up. One day you'll understand."

"Sure," Ethan said. He looked over at his pony vacant of any rider. "Hey Uncle Josh, Can I ride now?"

Josh waved for Ethan to come, and Ethan took off. Cade chuckled and limped back toward the cottage house.

He spotted Jenny at the corner of the barn talking to a group of people. She smiled and laughed as someone must have said something funny.

He wasn't sure what he'd been thinking when he'd decided to extend his stay. What he could be certain of though, was if he wasn't careful he may find Jenny crashing into more than his motorcycle. He didn't know if his heart could withstand another collision.

CHAPTER 18

Jenny waved as the last person drove down the lane, leaving the stables empty. Sarah stood in the doorway. Her hair was pulled back in a long ponytail and her face unusually pale. "That's the last of them," Sarah said.

"Amen to that," Jenny said. She'd been on her feet since the early hours of the morning giving tours in both the rescue and clinic facilities. But whatever exhaustion she felt didn't compare to tiredness she saw on Sarah's face.

"Why don't you head on into the house; I'll take care of the chores tonight."

"All of them?"

"I've got Josh to help." Or at least she'd seen him a little while ago tending to the ponies. She was sure she could convince him to stay a bit longer and help throw down some hay.

"If you're sure ..." Sarah lingered at the doorway.

Jenny rolled her eyes. "Didn't I just say so? Now off with you into the house before I have to call Michael and tell on you."

Ethan trailed Josh inside the barn.

"Ethan you take your Mom to the house while Uncle Josh helps me put the horses to bed for the night." Jenny glanced at Josh, waiting for him to protest.

Josh shrugged. "Sure, I ain't got no place to go tonight."

"Come on Mom, I'll help make supper." Ethan took Sarah's hand and led her out of the barn. She looked back over her shoulder at Jenny and Josh. Jenny shooed her with her hands like an old mother hen.

With Sarah out of the barn, Jenny turned to Josh. "You toss down the hay and I'll get started on the grain."

Josh stared at her long and hard.

"What?"

He shook his head and strode down the aisle headed for the hayloft.

Carefully, she weighed and measured each horse's ration of grain. Down at the last stall, the stallion snorted at her. To say he was the ugliest horse she'd ever seen would be an insult to the word. His buckskin coat was plastered with manure and his mane a tangled mess of hay and saw dust. Why anyone would want him this state was beyond her.

The Lord does not look at the things man looks at. Man looks at the outward appearance, but the Lord looks at the heart.

Perhaps it was good that this verse from Samuel had popped into her head. Apple, named after his favorite treat, turned and looked at her. His big brown eyes always so alert. Beyond the muck and the tangles was a warm heart beneath the flesh. Would there ever be a place in this rough tough stallion's heart to trust and love again?

Apple shook his head at her and banged the stall door with his foot. No doubt, he'd become impatient, waiting for his supper. She'd never opened his stall door without anyone else standing there beside her.

In the time that he'd come to the rescue, they'd managed to get him to wear a halter. It had been obvious from day one that Apple didn't like women, or that he'd been abused by one. Josh never did say where he'd found Apple.

Apple jerked his head as Jenny pulled the latch on the stall door. Normally, they'd toss his grain between the bars into his corner feeder. Slowly, she pulled the stall door to the side.

"Easy boy," she crooned. "I'm just going to feed you."

Apple snorted. He struck out his front foot. She stood inside the door's track and held out the bucket. "See, I'm not going to hurt you. Want some grain boy?"

What was she doing? Her heart skipped beating, her breath held in her lungs. She reached out the bucket a little further.

Apple swung his head back and reared. She didn't move. She waited—breath held.

Front feet stamped back down into the sawdust, Apple glared at her. He snorted and jerked his head.

She held fast to the bucket.

Slowly, Apple stretched out his neck toward the bucket. Jenny breathed, relieving the burning in her lungs. Mere inches from the bucket, Apple twitched his lips. He brushed his teeth on the edge of the bucket. Jenny waited. As he ran his teeth along the bucket, her fingers slipped and the bucket tilted forward. Apple ripped the bucket from her hands and reared back. He spun around and both back feet flew out towards her.

Two hands grabbed her by the shoulders and jerked her back. The stall door slammed shut and the latch turned before she could blink.

Josh growled in her face. "What did you think you were doing?"

"I..I ..." Jenny stammered. "I was trying to feed him."

"Feed him? Looked to me like you were trying to get yourself hurt. You know he's wild," Josh said.

"Well he won't ever be anything but wild unless somebody works with him!" Jenny clenched her fist, her heart pounding in her chest. Apple squealed and kicked at the side boards in his stall.

"He's Cade's problem, now. Not yours," Josh said.

Apple snorted at Josh's statement.

Jenny bit her lip, kicking at the sawdust she turned away.

From behind, Josh wrapped his arms around her and rested

his chin on her shoulder. "You want to talk about it?"

Jenny tried to laugh, but the tears slipped down her cheeks before she could catch them. "No."

"Men are like wild horses, you just can't trust us."

Jenny sniffled. Somehow, her brother always knew what was really bothering her. How did he always know? Maybe because they were twins, or maybe because they were always so close. Either way she wiped away the tears, turned, and looked at him.

"Married boyfriends, demolished motorcycles, and wild horses." She sighed, "What next?"

"There's always Cade Sheridan," Josh said.

"What about him?" Jenny sniffled back the last of her tears.

"Don't know, kind of funny don't you think that he'd have no family and no place to go?"

Jenny nodded. She had thought about that. He hadn't as much as protested when she dropped him off at the cottage house. Not that she'd given him any choice in the matter. And then there had been Cade's reaction to that Bailey guy today. They knew each other and it wasn't on friendly terms. She couldn't help wonder why. Then another thought struck her: if Cade was winning in the rodeo, why did he leave?

What business was it of hers?

Maybe, just maybe, if she'd made more of Brad's life her business she wouldn't have been so jilted by his announcement. Getting kicked by Apple would have felt better than the blow to her heart.

She thought she knew him, knew enough to love him, but obviously it had all been a lie. Did Brad's wife know of his sin? Mentally, she made a note to write the woman in Indiana a letter. If it were her, she'd want to know. How hard would it be to find an address? She didn't have a name, but she wouldn't let that stop her.

She realized, as she stood there wrapped up in her own thoughts, that Josh stood waiting. "Why aren't you going anywhere tonight?"

"What, and miss Sarah's meatloaf?" Josh teased.

Gently, Jenny elbowed him in the ribs as they walked down the stable aisle. "After a long day like this, I think tonight it will be take-out."

"If you lend me your car, I'll head into town and rustle up some pizzas from Joe's place."

Jenny paused. "So that's why you're staying home tonight."

Josh shrugged. "Maybe."

"What happened to the truck?"

"It takes more than fumes to get down to the auction house on a Saturday night."

"My keys are inside the glove box. Just give me a minute and I'll give you enough cash to pick up the pizzas."

CHAPTER 19

Cade stepped his left foot up on the bottom rail of the outdoor correl. He leaned forward, resting his elbows on the top rail and peeling an apple with a pocketknife. Sticky juice ran down the side of his hand. One chuck at a time he slivered off the apple and took small bites.

Inside the corral, Apple, the wild stallion, raced around in circles. The unruly buckskin breaking into a series of bucks before lapping again in a dead run around the wooden barrier.

He took another bite of his apple. Sarah assured him she wouldn't need the corral today, or even the next day. It hadn't taken much to talk Josh into helping him chase Apple from his stall and out into the outdoor corral. Together they placed a gated trail down the aisle of the barn and out the door into the corral.

He gazed now at the u-shaped stables. The corral was built snug between three sides of the stable. All the other horse stall doors kept shut as to not have Apple disturb them. Eventually, Apple would get tired of running.

He'd been trapped for so long, he needed to be free. It was the same way Cade had felt about Crystal and the rodeo.

He would have enjoyed the opportunity to own a good horse

like this, but what would he do with a horse? He watched Apple skid to a halt, the stallion's sides heaving for breath like a runner coming to a stop after a 5k.

These days it didn't take much to stir up old memories. He should never have come here. Something about this place stirred up memories and made him think about things that a man like him shouldn't think.

He spotted Jenny walking down Silver Wind's lane. He liked seeing her in a pair of ripped jeans and dark orange blouse.

He turned away and focused on Apple. He sliced another piece of the delicious fruit and watched as Apple stood, heaving, and staring. Cade clucked, held out the piece of fruit, and Apple shook his head.

"You sure now? Taste mighty fine." He tempted the horse again by holding out the apple slice on his hand.

Apple snorted.

Cade ate the apple and worked on cutting another piece. From the corner of his eye he watched Jenny approach. He hadn't seen her, not even at supper with the Wolfe family, for the past three days.

He'd followed the same routine, each day starting out with an apple for Apple. He visited the stables and stood by Apples stall, peeling and cutting an apple. The stallion ignored him first, but not able to resist the temptation of the sweet smelling fruit he'd been named after.

He supposed he should have been surprised to find out from Josh that it had been Jenny who gave the stallion such a ridiculous name. Apple ... he snorted, and so did the stallion. He felt a bump against this arm, and warm lips ran over the side of his hand. He ignored the stallion and continued to work his knife into the apple and cut out another wedge.

Jenny's boots crunched in the gravel of the driveway behind him. Apple's head jerked up and showed teeth, Cade pulled back away, stepping off the rail and out of Apple's reach.

He turned toward Jenny, as Apple took off in another lap

around the corral.

Why was it that a woman always seemed to make things difficult in this life?

"What is he doing out here?"

"Well good morning to you too," Cade said.

He gave her a moment to pout. Her lower lip tilted out slightly more than the other. She didn't have on make-up this morning,
the first that he'd ever seen her, and he liked seeing her natural
without the cosmetics. She had a peck of freckles scattered across
her cheeks and the bridge of her nose.

He'd never seen those before either, but found them attrac-
tive. He noticed she'd left her hair hang loose today to grazing
just below her ears.

He turned back to Apple, taking another lap around the correl. He had no business looking at Jenny or wanting to.

"It won't be easy getting him back into his stall for supper."

"We've switched his stalls. He'll take the one over yonder."
Cade pointed, "This way we can let him out every day to get
some exercise. Horses need to run. Otherwise they can be a real
handful to control if they're locked up all the time."

"I take it you've discussed this with Sarah?"

Cade nodded, "We'll let him out each day to run a while and
get used to his new freedom, then in about a week I'll start working on his halter skills. In the meantime, we're getting to know
each other."

Apple wondered over near Cade, he sniffed and jutted out a
lip reaching for the apple on the post near Cade.

"I can see that," she said, as Apple swiped the apple and took
off.

Cade shrugged, "You're out of the office early today, another
long lunch?"

He would never admit to her that it had been nice having her
along for the ride to pick up Sheldon, the surrendered Belgian
horse last week. She'd shown far more compassion than he had
inside him, for the old man, yet part of him felt it deep down.

That pang of loss, yearning for the past, and had been unable to respond.

"This came in the mail. I thought you might like to have it." Jenny held out an envelope to him. He took it, looked at the return address, then folded it up and stuck it in his back pocket.

"Aren't you even going to open it?"

"No need."

Jenny rolled her eyes at him. "If you want I can take you in town tomorrow. I'm sure we can find some places within a reasonable distance to get you a new motorbike."

Cade looked back at Apple, munching on some hay in the far end of the corral. He glanced back at Jenny. "If I didn't know better, I'd think you were in a hurry to get rid of me."

She ignored the remark, and kept talking. "Tomorrow then." She drew her shoulders back and her spine went straight as a pin.

"It's a date," Cade said.

She pushed back a wisp of red hair and tucked it behind her ear. "We'll leave first thing in the morning."

"You're at least going to allow me to eat breakfast first?" He teased, "Should I pack too?"

Jenny blanched. He shouldn't have said that, but it was too late to go take it back now. He reminded her that she'd done wrong, and to a woman like Jenny it ate at her soul until she couldn't stand looking at it—him.

She turned without a word and walked back down Silver Wind's lane. He stared at her until she disappeared around the bend of the stables. He gulped down a dose of fresh air and turned back to watching Apple finish off the last of the hay on the ground.

That night, Cade became restless in the little cottage house. Josh, like usual, was nowhere around. When he flipped on the television he got two channels – the news and a local high school rodeo. He flicked off the television and searched for a good book. There were no book shelves or books, for that matter.

He should have enjoyed the opportunity to unwind watching a

few good rides from the local boys at the rodeo, but his heart no longer held a thread to his old way of life. Although, a simple thing like touching a halter, or the smell of leather, horse flesh, and saddle soap gave him that yearning to be back in the saddle again.

How long before he could think about his old life without a stirring of grief in his heart, he didn't know. Nor did he know why God had brought him here.

He could have been smashed to smithereens by that truck, but he'd been saved, like the day he'd walked down into Olson's pond and was baptized when he was fourteen. It was the last time he'd seen his Momma and Daddy standing so proud.

A seizure of grief pained his heart. It all came down to that. His father's death hadn't been easy on any of them. Cade hadn't made it any better. Being the oldest, he'd stalked off determined to fill his Daddy's shoes. The only thing he'd filled was a hospital bed.

CHAPTER 20

Morning dawned with fat clouds and heavy downpours. Jenny wouldn't deny they needed the rain, but she was hoping it would hold off until she took Cade into town and helped him find a new vehicle. Car shopping was no fun in the rain. She was about as happy as a wet cat by the time she found him standing in front of Apple's stall.

Fortunately, Apple had enough sense to go back in his stall. Seeing the stallion gave Jenny more of a reason to get a jump-start on the day. If she was going to show Michael that they could run this place without another hand she and Josh were going to have to buckle down and take on more responsibility while Sarah took care of Sarah and the boys.

She'd dove into her Bible this morning hoping to find enough inspiration to hold her strength for the challenges ahead. Lately, she'd grown weary in heart since moving over into Michael's isolated apartment above the clinic. Oh, it had its advantages of never being late for work, and its disadvantages of always being at work.

She admitted only to herself, that the isolation started to sink in after Brad left. She spotted the light on in the stable's office and slipped inside.

"There's hot coffee in the pot," Sarah said, "It'll take off some of the chill."

Jenny had worn her rain gear, but the water ran down her jacket and soaked into the legs of her jeans. She grinned, heading for the coffee pot, "You read my mind."

"Actually, it was Cade. He's been out here since four. The coffee was made when I got here and he'd already fed half the horses."

Jenny reached for a cup. "That was nice of him, but I wouldn't be counting on someone like Cade to be around all the time like this."

"Michael and I have been discussing having Cade stay on with us."

Jenny poured a steaming cup of coffee. She sprinkled in a packet of sweet and low and stirred with a plastic spoon. "What makes you think a guy like him is going to want to stay?"

Sarah crossed her arms above her big belly and stared at Jenny. "What is it about Cade that you don't like? This isn't like you to be so judgmental toward someone you hardly know."

"That's just." Jenny took a sip of hot coffee. She closed her eyes for a moment savoring the feel of the hot liquid sliding down her throat and seeping warmth into her cold fingers. "Here you are ready to sign the guy onto the place when you don't know anything about him."

"I know everything I need to know about Cade. If you feel you need to know more, perhaps you should spend more time getting to know him and less time moping over a relationship that could have never gone anywhere."

Jenny took another sip of her coffee. She held tightly to the heat radiating off the coffee mug. This morning she'd searched the scriptures seeking answers to her problems. She'd even written down a line or two by Paul, "Do not be anxious about anything, but in everything, by prayer and petition, with thanksgiving, present your request to God."

"I called her," Jenny confessed.

"Oh Jenny ..."

"I thought she should know." Fact was she'd wanted to know the truth, needed to know the truth, but the truth hadn't settled the hurt within her heart, nor had it stopped the tears from drenching her pillowcase that night.

"It wasn't hard to find her, I just Googled her and she came up in the computer. I just thought maybe ..."

"He's married Jenny, that won't change." Sarah's tone lowered and she eased herself out of the desk chair and waddled toward Jenny.

"Yeah, but they could have been divorced. I didn't give him a chance ..." She felt it now, the heart squeezing, throat clogging, nose stifling sensations reacting to her emotions. She didn't want it to hurt, but at the same time she did. At least if it hurt she would know that she'd loved.

"She's just a few years older. So sweet, they've got two kids – a boy and a girl. I didn't have the heart to tell her about me and Brad. I told her I was from the clinic and she had all sorts of questions about how Brad was and saying she can't wait for him to return."

It had broken her heart more to say, "He's moved on to a new job, but I'll pray he returns home soon." And she'd meant every word.

"Didn't you say he was going home?"

Jenny shrugged. She wouldn't let it get to her. "He lied. I know that now. Brad once told me he was born in Texas, according to his wife he was born in Kentucky."

Sarah scrunched up her nose and made a face. She reached for the coffee and Jenny pulled the coffee pot out of her grasp. "Caffeine for the baby?"

"It's decaf."

"You just had to go and ruin my morning," Jenny teased, hoping to resolve the problems of her heart by sundown.

Yet the only ache she felt was the one that Cade caused in her belly and any thought of him made it go sour. Why did it always seem that Cade had the uncanny ability to jump into her mind when she tried so hard not to focus on him?

She took another long draft of her coffee hoping the scorching liquid would shed her heart ache and spread a new physical sensation in her chest, rather than the fluttering as Cade stepped into the doorway.

There was nothing worse than not having a ride, than being stuffed into Jenny's little two door sedan. When he looked over and saw Sarah's car wasn't much larger, he shook his head. *Petite women with petite cars.*

He imagined Jenny sitting on the back of his motorcycle with her arms wrapped around him. Would she be afraid or would she howl to the wind with the thrill of the ride as Crystal once did? He didn't want to think of Crystal. He'd told himself he wouldn't ever think of his ex-wife again. But here she was invading his thoughts, and it wasn't as if he wanted her there, either.

He'd learned to let go of that part of his life long ago. Yet something about being here, being around Jenny, had stirred up a nest of hurt he'd long forgotten. He'd vowed never to love another woman again, so why was he even standing there looking at that pretty red head with that short circuit temper of hers? Oh, she kept it in reined in, but he could see it flare in those sharp green eyes. The woman was like a cat, graceful and poised with sharp claws waiting to scratch.

She took him into Shelbyville and he stopped by the local bank. As he stood in line, he pulled out his wallet. A piece of paper flittered to the floor.

Cade reached down and picked up the photo. He traced the worn edges with his fingertip. They looked so happy ... so in love.

What had they been thinking, getting married that young?

She'd been straight out of high school, and he'd come straight out of hell.

At least at the time, that's what it had felt like when Dad died. Nobody could have stopped him back then. Not even his mother. He blinked and coughed to open his constricted throat.

He should have never jumped on that horse, just like he should have never been standing in that chapel in Vegas.

He'd sure showed them, hadn't he?

He started slipping the photo back in this wallet and paused.

What had he proved, if nothing at all, he felt empty.

He pulled out the photo and looked at it one more time. What right did she have to take away their happiness?

His fist curled around the picture as he stared out through the front windows of the bank. A car drove down the street and a little boy fought his mother's hold as she led him down the sidewalk.

"Don't let go," he said. "Don't ever let go."

CHAPTER 21

Jenny hadn't said anything when he came out, but her curiosity gave her away. Just like a cat.

They passed several car dealerships and each time Cade shook his head. "You won't find any Harley's there."

Jenny's shoulders sagged. They drove out of town, jumping up onto the highway and heading north. Soon, they passed a familiar spot and his ribs ached. The skid marks of his motorbike across the pavement were still there.

Jenny's lips tilted down in a frown as she looked onward to the deep gashes into the sod between the two different lanes. She looked over at him briefly and tried to smile, there was nothing happy about the place they'd just passed. Not in his book.

He'd gotten up that morning and flipped through his Bible. He couldn't seem to settle on a particular passage, that is until he came upon the first book of Samuel. Intrigued by David, he'd read about David's struggles with King Saul. But David had stood up and proved his bravery. He hadn't needed to read the rest of the passages through second Samuel to know that David too, had his faults and during his life time fell out of the grace of God.

Is that how God saw him after walking away from a marriage that would have never worked?

He wouldn't think of that now. It was over and so was his marriage. Now he would look ahead to the day. *This is the day that the Lord has made, rejoice, and be glad in it.* Remembering that verse from way back as a child made him smile.

"What's so funny?" Jenny asked.

"Nothing." She wouldn't understand.

All scrunched up in her tiny car, He figured it was about time he knew something about her – other than she broke up with a guy on the day the trailer slammed into the back of his motorcycle.

"There's a Harley Davidson dealership down here on the right. I'm sure you can find something there or they can get you want you want so you can be on your way."

Cade eyed her. Pink pouty lips, a little plump, but she radiated with style. He couldn't deny his attraction, but could deny falling into the trap of the temptation. He would be gone soon. Didn't she just say she was in a hurry to be rid of him?

They pulled into the Harley Davidson dealership. He uncurled his long legs out of her car and stretched. She waltzed right inside and started looking over the merchandise. Cade stuck his hands in his pockets and walked in behind her. He would need a new helmet, black like the old one. But as he picked one up off the stand, he yearned for his old Stetson. They didn't sell those in a dealership like this.

"Can I help you?" A burley looking guy with tattoos up his arm and a leather vest approached him.

Cade turned and the man offered his hand. "I'm looking for a new ride."

"Well, ya came to the right place. I'm Jake and I own this place."

"Cade, and this is Jenny." Cade introduced Jenny and she stepped up beside him to shake the man's hand.

"Will ya be trading anything in?" Jake asked.

"Not unless you take bikes in pieces," Cade said, trying to make a joke. By the expression on Jenny's face, she didn't think it was funny.

"Got into a fender bender did ya?" Jake chuckled, "I can't say we take 'em in pieces but we definitely can get you something whole again. Have anything in particular in mind?"

"Fat Boy."

Jenny gasped. Cade chuckled, "It's a motorcycle."

She nodded and Jake patted his belly, "Thought he was talking about me didn't ya?"

"Well, ya might be in luck, I've got one here but there's a guy who put down payment on it already. If he don't come through I can sell it to ya, or I can make some phone calls and see what I can find." Jake motioned for Cade and Jenny to follow him across the show room.

Outside through the tall glass windows, rain pelted and ran down the glass.

Cade circled the motorcycle and whistled low under his breath. "She's dressed out nice. There's a lot of chrome here, custom pipes and leather saddlebags. "

"She's a beauty," Jake held onto the motorcycles handlebars.

"I'm not much into orange," Cade told Jake. "I'd prefer black."

Jenny rolled her eyes and looked away. She stood clutching her purse strap and trying not to act as if she were paying attention to him.

"Why, so somebody can hit you in the night because they can't see you?" Jenny made a strangled sound in her throat. "What is it with you guys who drive around in black leather on black bikes and expect everyone to see you and not get hit?"

"If I remember correctly, you hit me in broad daylight," Cade said.

"She hit ya? Man, this is got to be good. Think twice about making the little woman mad uh?" Jake teased.

Jenny looked sharply at Jake, "I'm not his little woman."

"Ya mean ya two aren't?"

Cade shook his head, "She'd like to think so, but the truth is she's the reason I'm without my ride."

"Wow, I just assumed ya two were like married. And you're not even together?" Jake waved his finger between them.

"We're not married, dating, or otherwise acquainted." Jenny assured Jake.

"Not even friends?" Cade said, running his hands down over the seat of the Fat Boy. He took hold of the handlebars, itching to straddle all that chrome. But orange or not, it was somebody else's motorbike. He'd been too late, late, like the night he'd walked in on his wife in bed with one of his roadies at the truck stop motel.

He took a deep breath and tried to focus on the motorbike, but it was Jenny's response that brought him out of his stupor.

"I guess you could say we're friends." She begrudgingly admitted.

Jake ribbed Cade, "I've had a few friends like that too, only I married her and then she run off and here I am."

"I'm so sorry to hear that," Jenny told him, "But I assure you that is not the case with Cade and me."

Jake turned to Cade and changed the subject, "You sure it's got to be a Fat Boy? I've got a real nice Sportster here that I just got in on trade a few days ago."

Cade shook his head, "Anything else?"

"Just what you see here in the showroom." Jake rubbed his jaw, "You know I've got a v-rod just came in. Plain but she's straight from the factory. Could spruce her up a bit and customize her. Otherwise, I can make some calls, see if I can find a black Fat Boy ..."

"I'd appreciate that," Cade said, his heart set.

"V-rod, Fat Boy, Sportster what difference does it make? It's just a motorbike," Jenny said.

Both men looked at her.

"What color is the V-rod?" Jenny asked.

"Well it's black, "Jake said.

"See it's black. You want black, right? Maybe you should take a look at it," Jenny said. "You can customize here in your shop, yes?" She asked Jake.

"Yeah, have to order the parts and all, but won't take as long as having to find or order the motorbike," Jake said.

Cade looked at Jenny's determined face. "Fine, we'll take a look." Was she that desperate to get rid of him?

One look at the V-rod and Cade wasn't convinced.

"Now look at this sweet ride," Jenny said, walking around the bike and running her hand across the handlebars like a game show host assistant. "Nice leather seat …" she patted the seat, "and just look at that chrome. Who needs to customize it?"

"I do," Cade talked a few minutes with Jake and grabbed a card with info before turning to leave."

Back outside, standing in the pouring down rain, Jenny stood with her hands on her hips. "It couldn't have been a V-rod could it? It just had to be a black Fat Boy?"

"What can I say, I'm a man who knows what he wants." Silently, he added, *you*.

CHAPTER 22

Sundays at Silver Wind were a day reserved for family. For one day a week, the Wolfe family attended church and had dinner together without the Anderson twins. Jenny and Josh made their routine visit home to worship and catch up with their parents for the week. Their parents had no other children, and their mother looked forward to seeing them. Josh on the other hand, didn't seem to accept the importance of keeping their family ties together, not since Sarah had chosen Michael over him.

Jenny drove her little sedan over and parked in front of the carriage house where Josh and Cade stayed. Josh's truck and trailer were absent. She knocked on the door, anyway. Cade opened the door in nothing more than a pair of jeans.

Jenny's face turned aflame and she quickly glanced away.

Cade chuckled, "You rang?"

Jenny peeped over at him, staring at his broad chest for a long moment before settling her gaze on his bemused face. "I k-knocked," she said, looking away again.

"It's a little early to go shopping and most dealerships aren't open on Sunday's," Cade said. He leaned against the door jam.

"Is Josh here?" She still couldn't look at him.

"See his truck?"

"Know where he went?"

'Might," Cade said. "There something wrong?"

Jenny gulped. She closed her eyes, tilted up her face, and then snapped her eyes open determined not to look at his bare chest again. She gazed directly into his, laughing at her as they were.

"Could you please go put a shirt on?"

"Oh, right. Hold on a sec." Cade turned away and walked into living room. He disappeared into a bedroom. Jenny watched his back. She noticed he hadn't wrapped his bandages around his ribs, and a dark scar ran down the back of one shoulder.

Inside the leaving room, empty pizza boxes lay open and scattered over the coffee table and dirty clothes were thrown over the side of the couch. She stepped on something that crunched and from beneath her booted heel, she pulled peeled off a smashed soda can.

"This is so disgusting," she muttered, finding a moldy piece of pizza under an empty box as she collected them into a pile.

Cade walked back out of the bedroom pulling down a cotton shirt. "Sorry, the room service hasn't showed up yet."

"This isn't a motel."

"You're right, a motel room would have been cleaner. This place is really starting to stink."

"At least Josh cleans up after himself," Jenny said.

"That's because Josh isn't ever here to have to clean up." Cade countered.

She opened her mouth to reply then thought the better of it. She grabbed the pizza boxes and pushed past him into the small kitchen. "Where is my brother anyway? He was supposed to go with me."

Cade shrugged, "Beats me. Haven't seen him since last night."

Last night?" Jenny tossed the boxes in the garbage. "I'm sure he came home."

"He's a grown man, I don't think he needs a babysitter, do you?"

Jenny bit the inside of her lip. She strolled back out of the kitchen and headed for the door. "I could use a ride to church this morning."

It was as if he'd shot an arrow into her back. She spun around on her heel and stared at him. "And you expect me to take you?"

"Sure, or just hand me some keys to some wheels and give me some directions."

Jenny sighed, "Get in, I hope you like meatloaf."

The conversation around the Anderson's dinner table dried out as fast as the meatloaf Jenny's mother had prepared. Cade scooped up another bite of lumpy mashed potatoes and swallowed hard. Both Jenny's parents and Jenny kept glancing in his direction.

It wasn't Cade they were keeping watch on, but he fidgeted none the less, with the suspicion that he sat in Josh's seat.

"Didn't you tell your brother that dinner was at one o'clock?" Jenny's mother, whom he had been introduced to as Mary, asked her daughter.

"He knows, Mom."

Cade took a bite of meatloaf and hurried to gulp down half a glass of milk to wash it down.

"Let it go," Jenny's father, Bill, said.

Mary bristled and grabbed the pot of potatoes and took them to the kitchen. Cade sighed. He'd been sitting there praying the woman wouldn't push seconds on him.

"Apple pie anyone?" She returned with a fresh baked pie that he feared she'd baked herself.

"Cade?" She held the pie under his nose.

"No thank you. I couldn't eat another bite," he said.

Mary appeared taken back. "Why you hardly touched your meatloaf."

"Cade doesn't eat much Mom. He's watching his figure." Jenny gave him a sly smile and he grinned.

"A man watching his figure? You all are pulling my leg," Mary put the pie plate on the table in front of Bill.

"I've heard a few the guys at work who have to watch their diets, cholesterol and all," Bill said, sticking his fork into the pie. Mary slapped his hand and gestured with her eyes toward Cade.

"Yeah, like Daddy said."

"I suppose I could wrap up a piece or two for Josh. I just made this pie ...." Mary trailed off oblivious to make them all feel guilty.

"Just let Daddy eat the pie, you know he's the only one who's gonna," Jenny said.

"Jennifer Renee ..."

Jenny rolled her eyes. "Come on Mom, I'll help you clean up."

He watched Jenny get up from the table and gather her plate and his. When she disappeared through the swinging door, Bill leaned back in his chair. "Jenny says you got yourself in an accident and now you're without a motorcycle."

"Yes sir," Cade replied.

"God's got plans for you, son. Mark my words, the way Jenny tells it you should have been dead the way that truck ran right over your motorbike like it was trash on the road. Miracle it was that you survived and my girl took you in."

Cade arched an eyebrow. "I consider myself very lucky." So, Jenny hadn't told her parents who was at fault for the accident.

Bill went on to say, "Had that girl all set up to work at my firm. Would have started her out as a junior accountant on the third floor, but she's a loyal friend. Don't know what they'd do over at that place they call Silver Wind if Jenny wasn't there to run the place."

Cade crossed his arms. Obviously, Bill hadn't ever taken a drive to visit his daughter and seen that Silver Wind was run by more than one person, and Jenny wasn't the one in charge. Even if, he got the feeling, she thought she was.

"You married?" Bill asked.

"Nope."

Bill nodded. "That's good. That Brad was bad from the start. But you know Jenny. She wouldn't listen to nothing we tried to tell her. Had to find out the hard way." Bill leaned forward and his voice dropped low, "You know she was expecting a marriage proposal the day he walked in and told her he was married. Nothing short of the Lord's doing that she came upon you the same day."

The kitchen door swung open and Jenny walked back in and picked up the apple pie.

"Now I was gonna have some of that," Bill whined.

"Josh is here, Mom says you don't need any pie. You need to start watching your weight along with the other guys in the office." She patted his belly and turned on her heel.

"Was only going to eat it to be nice," Bill mumbled.

Cade excused himself from the table and sought out Jen in the kitchen. Mary stood washing the dishes in the old fork and spoon themed kitchen. A lime wall clock ticked above the sink and Mary gave him a weary smile.

He spotted Jenny out on the porch and Josh with his hand out.

CHAPTER 23

"I'll pay you back as soon as I can."

Jenny had never seen Josh so anxious. A dark streak ran across his cheek from his run in with the pitchfork. And his eyes appeared redder than she'd ever seen them. Had he been crying?

Desperation laced his voice and tugged at a place in her heart. This was her brother; how could she tell him no?

"How much do you need?"

"Two hundred …A hundred at least …" he shifted from foot to foot.

"Two hundred?!?" her voice rose with the shock of his request.

"I know … I know … but even a hundred …"

"What do you need it for?" Jenny asked.

"I told you I'm out of gas for the truck. It's been a bad week and I had to pick up that horse over at the Gavin's."

Her arms prickled with goose bumps. She didn't believe him, but even as the chill trickled down her spine, she couldn't recall Josh ever telling a lie.

"Did you ask Sarah? The rescue has always reimbursed you for gas when traveling to rescue a horse."

"It's Sunday. Besides, the rescue reimburses me after I pick up the horse and fill out those ridiculous forms that you and her created."

He shoved his hands in his pockets and then pulled them out again. He grabbed her by the arms. "Please Jenny, I'll pay you back."

She couldn't say no to the pleading in her twin brother's eyes. "I'll have to write you a check."

"You don't have any cash?"

"Like I carry that much cash on me all the time, Josh. Do you want the money or not?" Jenny asked.

He frowned and nodded. "I'll wait here while you get it."

"You know you have to go in and say hi to Mom and Daddy or they'll never let you live it down. Especially, since you didn't show for dinner."

She reached for the back door and Josh scowled. "Just hurry up all right? I almost choked on the meatloaf last time and I'm not taking left overs home with me."

Before she could grasp hold of the doorknob, it opened. Cade stood holding the door. Her heart did a little a flutter and she ducked her head, walking past him to hide her smile. Josh pushed past her and headed toward the dining room.

Mary turned and followed him. "Josh dear, are you hungry?"

Jenny tried hard to ignore Cade's riveting stare. She reached behind the door as he closed it and grabbed her purse from the hook beneath her coat. She pulled out her checkbook laid it on the counter. Cade leaned back against the counter, crossing his arms s and his legs. He watched her and she felt his gaze like lead on her arms as she pulled out a pen and scribbled Josh's name across the top line of a check.

"Sure you want to do that?" Cade asked.

Jenny filled in the amount and shifted her stance to block his view from seeing the amount.

"Hit you up for gas money too, did he?"

Her pen slipped and a long ink line smeared across the edge of her check. She glanced up at Cade. "It's none of your business." She placed her pen on the next line, about to write and paused. "How do you know he needs gas money?"

Cade took the pen from Jenny's hand. "Sarah asked me to deliver him some cash yesterday, saying he needed gas money for today."

Why didn't Josh tell her that? Of course Josh wouldn't want to bother Sarah on a Sunday, but if she gave him gas money yesterday … Maybe Cade was mistaken, or maybe Sarah hadn't given him enough to fill both tanks in his truck. But his truck wouldn't need two hundred dollars' worth to fill …

Jenny glared at Cade. She snatched the pen back from him and voided the check. She ripped it from her checkbook and tore it in chunks. She started writing a new check.

What did Cade know, Josh was her brother and family was there to always help each other. Josh said he would pay her back and he would. How could she explain the connection she had with her twin to someone like Cade?

She finished signing her name and ripped the check out of her checkbook. Josh came back in the kitchen along with their mother. "You got that, Jenny? I've got to get going."

"I can pack you some leftovers. You're too thin these days," Mary complained.

"No Mom. I've got to go," Josh said, heading for the door.

"Then I'll see you on Sunday. Don't forget dinner is at one o'clock and it would be nice if you started coming back to services in the morning. That Johnson girl has been asking for you." Mary smiled that her cheeks plumped up and her eyes glistened with hope.

"I'll see what I can do," Josh reached for the check in Jenny's hand, but Cade took hold of it at the same time.

"That's mine," Josh said.

A vein twitched in the side of Cade's throat. Jenny tugged on the check, but Cade didn't let go.

"You've been using a whole lot of gas in the past few days," Cade said.

"That's what I do," Josh stared at Cade.

Jenny felt the tension grow thick between the two men. No doubt that her mother felt it too, as she looked away. Mary busied herself with tiding the countertop by the butternut stove.

"See that you pay it back. *All of it*," Cade said.

Josh yanked the check from their hands and stormed out the back door. Jenny shoved Cade out behind Josh.

Josh stalked off through the yard and around the side of the house out of sight. Cade stumbled back on the porch. Jenny slammed the door behind her. "Just who do you think you are?"

From the corner of her eye, she spied her mother peeking out the window. Her face burned along with her temper. She paced back and forth on the porch with her fist clenched. She tried counting to ten. She tried asking the Lord to help calm her down. She tried looking at Cade and biting her tongue, but the arrogant expression on his face infuriated her.

"What business is it of yours? This isn't your family! You're a guest in my parents' home and as such you can't interfere with family business."

Cade shoved his hands in his pockets. "Where I come from a man doesn't beg for money off his friends and family all within the same hour unless their up to no good."

"Needing gas for his truck is not up to no good!" She tried reigning in her temper.

"You don't think he gave your parents the same line while he was in there and you were out here writing him a check?"

"Josh wouldn't do that."

"What about the money Sarah gave him?" Cade asked.

"The rescue is financially strapped; it always has been. She probably didn't give him enough."

"And your parents probably didn't give him any either, right?"

She didn't want to talk about this anymore. She snapped her checkbook closed and stuffed it in her purse. She had half a mind to tell Cade he could walk home, but that would not be very Christ like.

"Listen, I don't know why your buttin' your nose in where it doesn't belong all of a sudden, but it's not your business."

"Your folks seem like real nice people. Family dinners are far and few between where I come from, you should cherish these Sundays and honor them."

"You don't think I don't know that?"

Cade moved close to her. He took her chin in his hand and tilted her face up to where her eyes met his. "I think, you think, that you know everything. And there are some things that none of us know and we've got to trust God that *He* knows best."

"You don't understand when it comes to Josh and me. We're twins. I know things that others don't know. I can feel it." She didn't know why she had to tell him that, but staring into his eyes made her dizzy and thrilled at the same time.

"Jenny ..." Her name was a husky murmur on his lips. She tilted her head further and his hand slid to the side of her throat. Her pulse throbbed beneath his thumb. He tipped his head forward, their noses touching in an Eskimo style kiss. She closed her eyes, waiting ...

"Oh heavens me ... I'm so sorry ..."

Both she and Cade broke apart at the sound of Mary's voice.

CHAPTER 24

He knew the moment she entered the yard. The buckskin stallion reared his head. A bucket of chopped apples dangled in his hand, and Apple tossed his head up, laying his ears back and showing his yellow stain teeth in Jenny's direction.

Cade stood stock still. After several days of being near the stallion, this day he'd slipped through the corral and stood inside with the jittery horse. He didn't dare flinch.

He smelled it, the heavy scent of her orchid perfume over the crisp freshness of the apples in the bucket. He smelled it standing in her mother's kitchen, too. He chided himself remembering how close he'd gotten and how that scent had branded itself in his memory.

She walked right up to the corral like she owned it. Didn't the woman have any sense of self-preservation? The stallion gauged her in his sight. A high-pitched warning rang in the air. Jenny stepped up on the first rung of the fence.

"Stay there," he said. Apple took off in a dead run towards the far end of the correl. He ground his teeth and strolled towards the intrusion. Her chin notched up an inch when he came near her. Her jeans pulled taunt across her wide hips, pulling denim fabric to turn white at the stress points. Her pink blouse would pale in comparison to her skin after being in the sun for an hour. All those freckles draping down her nose told him her fair skin didn't like being exposed.

He grunted, dropping the bucket. His ribs were healed enough that he no longer needed to wear his bandages, but they ached at the sight of her.

A strawberry stained brow lifted at his approach.

He halted within inches of her nose. She was as skittish as Apple.

He recognized the quick flash of red in her cheeks, but if she was uncomfortable, she didn't show it. He kept his body turned slightly towards the stallion. Apple pawed and flicked his tangled tail to keep the flies away.

"Surprised to see you're not over at the clinic."

"Sarah went with Michael, so I'm watching the rescue today." Jenny looked over his shoulder at Apple. "What are you doing in there?"

Her question irritated him. Was she that blind she couldn't see? Or was it that she simply didn't want to?

"My job until somebody interfered."

"If you're referring to me, I hardly stopped you from feeding Apple. As far as *your job* goes, that has yet to be determined," Jenny said.

No one in his life had ever irritated him and infatuated him at the same time as Jenny. He moved closer, grasping the top rail of the corral with both hands. "Three minutes ago that horse was eating out of my hand. Another minute or two and I might have gotten to touch him. Then you showed up, and ruined what progress I've made all morning."

"And you know that for a fact?" Jenny asked.

Behind him Apple snorted.

His sentiments exactly.

"Yeah, I do," Cade said.

"I'll have you know that I've been giving that horse apples for almost a year, and if he was going to let anyone touch him it would be me. After all, I named him."

Cade shook his head. "Apple's a real fine name for a spirited stallion."

She frowned. "You're making fun."

"Not at all," but he smiled at her in a way that she would have to be a fool not to know he was doing that indeed.

Out of the corner of his eye, he watched Apple. The stallion paced in a circle at the far corner. He wasn't going to get anywhere else with the animal while Jenny stood there.

"I came out here to talk to you, but I see that you'd rather be horsing around than in my company." She pouted with those pretty pink lips of hers.

"I thought we were talking all this time."

Jenny rolled her eyes. "There are other things that need done around here for you to be fooling around with Apple all day. You did tell Sarah you'd take the job, didn't you?"

He crossed his arms, "I did."

"Our next open house is next Saturday. There are quite a few horses who are adoptable or needing our attention that could be adoptable with a little more work."

His brows rose. He scratched his chin, feeling the stubble of growth from the day.

"What exactly do you want me to do?"

She grinned, like a cat that caught its prey. "Each horse needs to be groomed daily, stalls to be cleaned, and no less than twenty minutes spent giving each horse individual attention."

"Sounds like you need to get yourself a stable boy." He told her. "I'm just a trainer."

Her eyes changed to a vivid green, widening with his words. Her glossy pink lips drew taunt. She opened her mouth to speak, but stalked off towards the stables in silence.

Cade chuckled. So Josh hadn't showed up to do his job this morning, he thought. There was no way he was cutting her any slack, not where that brother of hers was concerned.

Apple plodded over to the bucket of apples. The stallion

snorted twice nudging the rubber container. Cade turned slow, keeping his eye on the horse. The stallion nodded and stuck his nose into the bucket.

Cade smirked. He didn't take orders from bossy red heads. He didn't take jobs that required him to stay in one place longer than a few weeks, either.

He turned his back to the eating horse and ducked out of the corral.

CHAPTER 25

Jenny flung another scoop of manure into the wheelbarrow. She admitted to herself that had she been a little more tactful with Cade, she might not have to stand there flinging horse manure on her own.

She wiped the sweat from her brow. This is what she got for asking for a little help.

Josh hadn't shown up and she hadn't seen him since Sunday. What did Cade know that neither Josh nor he was telling her?

Today should have been her day off, and if this all had been done she may have taken Cade motorcycle shopping this afternoon. Now, however, she doubted she'd make it to Bible study this afternoon, let alone have any time to finish writing down her answers to the last chapter's questions. Now she understood why Sarah never had her questions finished on time.

She took more advantage of her friend, running this rescue, than she cared to admit. Perhaps this is the lesson she needed. She decided to pitch in more often over here with the daily chores. It was obvious they couldn't relay on Josh, and Sarah's pregnancy had begun to restrict her from the physical aspects of running a stable. Sarah and Michael had been right to hire another hand, but Cade?

She grimaced at the blisters on her hands.

Why didn't she think to put a pair of gloves on? She gripped the handles of the wheelbarrow, heaving it up. Her sudden jerk sent the load tipping and the contents spilled out into the stable aisle. She sighed, closing her eyes and asking the Lord to help her find some patience.

The sound of a fork scrapping up her mess made her eyes open. She righted the wheelbarrow.

"I can do it." She reached for the pitchfork in Cade's hands. Cade grabbed her hand by the wrist. Her breath caught in her throat. His eyes narrowed on the red welts in the palm of her hand.

"There's balm in the tack room, put it on those blisters." He reached in his back pocket and threw a pair of glove at her. "And put these on."

She clutched the gloves with one hand and glared at him. He released her and turned away forking up the pile of manure at his feet.

Shrugging she mumbled, "Thanks" and walked toward the tack room. Silently, she thanked God too, for answering her prayer for help.

The balm made her blisters sting, but without it, they would have gone numb sooner and she wouldn't be able to continue cleaning stalls.

They worked together the rest of the day, cleaning stalls, grooming horses, and sharing a lunch worthy of a bunch of six-year-olds – peanut butter and jelly sandwiches. Jenny brought in the horses, grooming them one by one, while Cade played with the yearlings out in the west field. By evening all the horses were fed, bedded, and cared for, including Apple who willingly walked into his stall.

"They're not back yet," Jenny said, gazing out at the pink and orange smeared sky. She held out Cade's gloves to him, reluctant to admit what a good team they made working together.

"They probably stopped for dinner with it being this late." She checked her watch, heading down the lane. "It looks like you're on your own tonight," she called back to Cade.

A little pang of guilt struck her as she left him standing there by the stables. Cade Sheridan was a grown man; he could take care of himself. Somehow, it didn't make her feel any better leaving him.

During Bible study she couldn't focus. Twice Sally Mason asked her to lead them in the opening prayer and Sally herself ended their session rather than Jenny like usual. She tried hard to follow the lesson and comment on the materials, but Cade interrupted her thoughts.

Even on the drive home, she couldn't get him off her mind.

The lights were on at the cottage house when she returned home. The ladies' Bible study was the highlight of her week. Although the two-chapter assignment they were given brought an overwhelming sense of dread inside her.

There was no way Sarah could catch up by next week.

Looking down at her sore palms she wondered how she could stay caught up either.

It was time someone pulled the strings tighter around this place.

Spotting Josh's truck parked by the cottage, she pulled up in front of the little house. She marched up and knocked on the door. Not waiting for an answer, she went inside.

Cade stood in the kitchen. He looked freshly showered, his hair still damp and he wore a clean white t-shirt and a pair of flannel pants.

Jenny stumbled in the doorway. "Sorry." She winced at her error. "I forgot Josh isn't the only one living here anymore."

He stood poised with a carton of milk in his hand. She should have backed away and left, but she was no coward. And Cade was not her foe. She spied the pizza on the counter –Josh's favorite excuse for supper.

She picked up a slice. Mid way to her mouth, she paused as he gave her a strange look.

"Help yourself," he said.

She dropped the slice back into the box. Heat rose up her neck and flushed her cheeks. "Sorry, Josh always ...It's Josh's usual fare."

"So I've noticed."

"Is he here?" she asked wanting to kick herself for just barging in on him.

Cade shrugged.

"I saw his truck parked outside," Jenny said.

"I heard the shower go off a little while ago."

She headed though the house, noting on the way that some-one had picked up, and climbed the stairs to the upper level. She found Josh pulling on a clean flannel shirt in his room.

"Knock much?" Josh asked.

"Apparently not enough," she said taking a seat on the edge of his bed. She picked up the scattered papers on the coverlet and stacked them in a neat pile.

"I didn't think maid service was until next week."

"You couldn't pay me to clean up your slop around here," she said.

"Figured it was you who came in, cleaned the living room." Josh shrugged. "So what's up?"

"You're supposed to be helping at the rescue and instead you're never around."

Josh scratched the nap of his neck. His damp hair a shade darker than her own. His green eyes reminded her of dark moss from inside the forest at the edge of the farm. It was then she noticed his left eye had a black ring around it.

"I just picked up two horses for the clinic, Jenny. That's what I do." Josh turned and opened the drawer of his dresser behind him.

"Did one of them punch you in the eye too?"

He ignored her question.

"You're the foreman Josh, you can't leave Sarah to run every-thing," Jenny said.

"This was Sarah's idea remember?" Josh turned back straightening out a faded blue ball cap.

"And we agreed to help her. You're just sore because she married Michael." Jenny stood up and crossed her arms.

"How many times do I have to tell you that that don't bother me? If anything I think it annoys you!"

"Me? I'm not the one who offered to marry her."

"It was the right thing to do if ole Mike didn't come along. But whether I offered or not, doesn't mean that I've been itching to get hitched like you have." Josh pulled his cap down on his head.

"I have not."

"You're tellin' me that if Brad wouldn't have told you he was married that you wouldn't have been still waiting for a marriage proposal?"

"This has nothing to do with Brad. It's done and over with"

She hated that he'd done that to her. She tried so hard to pretend that it hadn't hurt, but even now the dull ache returned. She sniffed back unexpected tears and turned away.

She pressed the heel of her palms to her eyes and took a deep breath. Behind her, Josh rustled around with the papers on the bed.

When she turned back he was slipping something into his back pocket.

"I expect you over at the stables tomorrow. You should thank Cade for doing your job today."

Josh readjusted the bill of his cap. "I told you. I'll help you when I can. I don't see you over there every day mucking stalls."

"I didn't get these sitting at my desk at the clinic, now did I?" Jenny held out her blistered palms.

Josh walked past her to the closet where, after digging around for a few minutes, tossed a pair of gloves on the bed beside her. "Try wearing these next time."

"I shouldn't have to wear them at all. I'm tired of doing your job, Josh." Jenny didn't mean to yell, but how else could she make Josh listen?

"I don't got time for your lectures right now."

"Do you want Cade to take your job?" Jenny asked.

"Why not, Sarah hired him to work with the horses, he might as well clean up after them too."

Jenny scooped up the gloves and followed Josh down the hall. "Where are you going?"

"Auction tonight, maybe I can pick up some business." Josh headed down the stairs. "I need the cash."

He walked across the living room and reached for the door.

"I'm not worried about you paying me back."

"Good," Josh said, opening the door and walking out and shutting the door in Jenny's face.

She turned and ran into Cade. He blocked her path to reopening the door. She glared up at him. His dark penetrating gaze sent a shiver down her spine. Tiny flecks of gold stared back at her, and for a moment she forgot how much she didn't like him. She couldn't trust him. He was a drifter.

So why was he still here?

"I see you got yourself a pair of gloves."

"No thanks to Josh." Jenny made a motion to step around him, but Cade didn't budge. She crossed her arms. "If you'll excuse me I'd best be going."

Cade stepped out of her way. "Don't forget to say your prayers tonight." Jenny yanked open the door and stepped outside. "You're going to need them," he said.

CHAPTER 26

People arrived shortly after nine o'clock to the rescue on that Saturday morning. Sarah and Jenny walked around dressed in their purple polo shirts, and they'd gone so far as to give him one of his own. Underneath the Silver Wind Logo was his trainer status. He felt like a personal fitness trainer off those infomercials he'd watched on television in the cottage.

It came as no surprise to him that people from all across the state flocked to Silver Wind for their monthly open house. Sarah and Jenny took turns giving tours of both the rescue and the clinic. A large lock box hung mounted on the wall near the stable office marked, "Donations."

Cade kept close to the horses.

There were nine horses in their stalls, eight adoptable. Many of the other horses were out grazing in the fields and the ponies raced around the corral. It made a beautiful sight for those driving up to the rescue to see the place in full bloom.

Over the past weeks he'd gotten to know each of the horses' personalities. It was his business to know, his duty at Silver Wind to acquaint himself with the horses. He'd started before Sarah and Michael had offered him the job.

Silver Wind wasn't like any place he'd ever been. He didn't set down roots in places for very long, but here he didn't feel in a rush to be leaving anytime soon.

The Wolfe family welcomed him to their table like one of their own. Occasionally, Jenny joined them, and sometimes Josh.

Josh didn't snore, but there was something about him that reminded Cade of himself not long ago. He noticed someone coming in and cleaning the cottage despite his efforts. The kitchen counters smelled of citrus and the stainless steel sink sparkled.

He tried to imagine Jenny doing his laundry and making his bed. The black bound Bible on his bed gave her away.

By noon the coffee and donuts were replaced with punch and cookies. Cade took each horse out in the corral to have their turn at freedom from the stuffy crowd. He answered questions, and demonstrated each horse's best attributes.

He watched Josh, who showed up late in the morning, cart off a group of visitors on tour. The little Morgan mare plodded beside him. He wove through the people standing in the aisle. He heard the impact of a hoof slamming into a door. He neglected to tend to Apple, so far that day.

Every day he let the stallion out of his stall. His persistence had paid off last evening when he slipped a brand new red halter over Apple's head. He would check on Apple next, having not a minute all morning to check on the rowdy stallion.

Of course a man like Bill Bailey would want to get his hands on a horse like Apple.

With the Morgan safe in its stall, Cade made his way toward Apple. He spotted Jenny with a clipboard hugged close to her chest.

Immediately, Cade recognized Bailey standing in front of Apple's stall. He had a lot of nerve showing up back here, thought Cade.

Bill Bailey stood two inches less than six feet. His broad shoulders and wide grin made her feel like a schoolgirl again. His wide brimmed hat tilted back away from his high forehead, and he wore a belt buckle the size of Nebraska. It gleamed when the light touched it. Even the tips of his boots shone with gold winged tips.

From the moment he walked up to her, his wit charmed her. He was nothing like Cade would have her think of him.

He made her laugh, and before she realized it she offered to give him a personal tour around the stables. They ended up back here, in front of Apple's stall.

"He's a real prize," he drawled.

"Apple?" Jenny smiled. "Cade's been working with him. Soon he might just lead, but it will take a long while before he can be ridden."

Bailey frowned. "Is that so? Figured Cade would have pushed off a while back."

Apple backed up in his stall and laid his ear back. The horse's unease did not fail to cross her attention. She dismissed it. Apple wasn't the friendly sort of horse, anyway.

But the interest in Bailey's eyes was unmistakable. She had several applications filled out on her clipboard for several of the other horses. With fall coming, it would serve the rescue's resources well to have several of the horses adopted before it snowed. They would get loving new homes and Sarah's burden would be eased.

They were near full capacity and with a few more stalls empty, they wouldn't have to turn anyone away. Most of their surrendered horses had come during the winter months.

Bailey gripped the bars on the stall door and peered in at the wayward stallion. Apple tossed his head. The crash of the front door vibrated through the dirt floor beneath Jenny's feet.

"Cade's been working with him, uh?" Bailey rubbed his hand over his chin. "Hasn't made much progress, has he?" Bailey turned back to Jenny, unaffected by Apple's outburst. "How about you just name your price and I'll take him off your hands right now."

"I'm afraid it doesn't work like that here."

Bailey reached in this back pocket.

Nervously, Jenny continued, "Application first, there's a two hundred and fifty-dollar fee on approval, and a minimum of three visits to make sure you and the horse will get along—that is when he's available for adoption."

Bailey wiggled his dark brows at her, "I'm sure we'll get along just fine." He leaned in close to her.

Her heart raced.

"Why don't you fill out an application," she turned the clipboard in his direction. Pulling a pen from the top clip she held it out to him. "You seem like a nice enough guy. I'm sure with Cade working with him, Apple will be ready for adoption in a few months."

Bailey slipped his business card under the clip of the board along with several hundred dollar bills. "A horse that's been trained by another man is of no use to me, darlin'."

"We can start you and Apple's first visit in just a few weeks," jenny said, staring down at the wad of cash on the board.

"Why don't I just stop in later this evening when this here is all over and pick up the stallion? This way I'll give him a real nice home and train him, and you all will have one more stall open for another horse that needs your help."

Jenny pulled back the clipboard. She picked up the cash and held it out to Bailey "I can't accept this Mr. Bailey. It wouldn't be right."

"Consider it an early donation," Bailey said.

"If you want to stop by tomorrow …"

"Don't waste your time," Cade cut her off.

"Excuse me?" She spun around and ran into Cade's chest. He grasped her arms to steady her and she shrugged him off.

"This horse isn't adoptable." Cade glared over Jenny at Bailey

Jenny felt her spine stiffen and she pulled back her shoulders, standing between the two men.

"I believe this is between the lady and me." Bailey told Cade.

"And I believe I told you once before not to waste your time on trying to get your hands on this stallion, Bailey. He's not leaving here anytime soon, and he's not leaving here with you."

"You don't know when to mind your own business do you, Sheridan? Didn't learn your lesson after all this time, I see."

Jenny glanced back and forth between the men.

"I could say the same about you," Cade placed his hand on Jenny's shoulder. She glanced back at him.

"I think you need to let me handle this," she said.

"Yeah, Sheridan, don't you have some kids waiting to be led around on a pony outside or something?" Bailey grinned at him.

"This isn't over." Cade told Bailey as he released Jenny, "That horse isn't adoptable." The cold tone of Cade's voice sent goose bumps down her arms. From inside the stall, Apple nipped at the bars of the stall door. Bailey jerked his hands back from reach.

"You let me know when I can pick this fellow up, just don't wait too long, you hear?"

Jenny watched Bailey walk away, leaving her standing there with the money in her hand. Her mood turned from peach to black before he disappeared out of the stables.

She found Cade in the feed room, weighing out the evening rations in preparation for later.

"You might work here now, but Sarah and I still make the decisions on what horses are adoptable."

Cade took another scoop of feed and poured it in scales. "Apple's not adoptable, especially to a man like Bailey."

"Is or is not, Apple in the barn with the rest of the horses that are available for adoption?" She asked tucking clipboard under her arm.

"Apple doesn't get turned out with the rest of them. You know that better than anyone." Cade pulled the clipboard from beneath her arm. He flipped through the hundred dollar bills beneath the clip and yanked them out. "Is this what you call a good home?"

He held up the bills in her face. "It's dirty money. Is that the kind of place you want people thinking Silver Wind is?"

"You don't like him."

"You think?" Cade asked. He poured the feed off the scale and into a large clear measuring cup.

"Bailey is a gentleman, which is more than I can say about you." Jenny grabbed for the cash.

Cade pulled the money out of reach. "That's a hefty sum for a gentleman to pay for just a tour."

Jenny's jaw went slack. She sputtered searching for the right words to say. Cade took another scoop of feed and poured it on the scale.

"It ... It was a-a donation," she said.

Cade bunched the money into a fist. "Let me tell you about Bailey. I've seen his type before. I know his type, and sweetheart, he's far from nice. Men like Bailey want horses like Apple for one reason. They like them wild and untamed, otherwise he can't use them to gain profit."

"Adopted horses can't be trained and resold, it's in the adoption contraction," Jenny said. He hackled her defenses.

"No one said he would sell the horse," Cade handed her back her clipboard. "I know you want the best for Apple, but handing him off in the condition he's in now isn't in Apple's best interest. You might think you know everything, but trust me on this one. You give Apple to Bailey, then these last few weeks that I've spent working with him would have been for nothing."

"What did Bailey mean when he said about you learning your lesson?"

Cade shoved a scoop into a feedbag and turned back toward Jenny. "It was a long time ago, and I'd rather it be left in the past where it belongs."

"You don't think Bailey would train and break Apple?" She wanted to understand. For a second his facial expression softened and felt as if he would open up to her, but within a blink of her eye that softness vanished.

"Oh he'll break 'em. If you're lucky, he may even give him back after he's done."

"You act as if the man abuses horses on a regular basis."

"He's a dealer. Horses are his business. The fact that he came back here a second time and tried to buy you off says he's up to no good."

"You're prejudiced because of your past."

"What's going on here?" Sarah stepped into the feed room. "I can hear you two arguing in my office. You're making the visitors nervous, not to mention the horses."

"Ask her." Cade flicked the money down at Jenny's feet and stepped around Sarah.

Jenny reached over and picked up the money.

"What was that all about?" Sarah asked.

"If you don't fire him, I will."

"Now why would we do that? Cade is wonderful with the horses, and a big help around here." Sarah said.

Jenny clipped the money back on the board and handed it to Sarah. "Come on, Sarah you just saw how he talked to me. He's rude, arrogant, and he just tried to prevent Apple from adoption."

"It sounded more like to me that he tried to prevent Apple from being adopted by the wrong person," Sarah said.

"This has been Mr. Bailey's second visit to our open house to see Apple. One more visit and that counts toward the adoption."

Sarah hugged the clipboard to her chest above her rounded belly. "It only counts if he's filled out and signed an application for a horse that is available for adoption. Cade got a halter on Apple last night. You know horses don't train overnight."

"I don't know why I even try." Jenny threw her hands up.

"Every horse that comes here needs something from us." Sarah laid the clipboard on a stack of hay "Horses aren't like people. They can't tell us what they need, but we eventually figure it out. Some horses are here longer than others. People can be the same way. You need to wait and find the right opportunity to work out your differences with Cade."

Jenny shook her head. Cade Sheridan didn't present himself as a man looking for an opportunity. He was a drifter. A man

with no ties, no family, and no connections to anything permanent. Maybe it was time someone latched onto him and led him
in the right direction.

She'd have a better chance with a stubborn mule, although it
might be fun to yank on his lead a time or two. Then she would
leave the rest up to God to close the gate on him.

CHAPTER 27

The aroma of fried chicken curled a finger under his nose and drew him toward the dining room. All the trimmings of a true KFC dinner were laid down the middle of the big cherry-varnished table.

Cade ruffled the small dark head of Ethan devouring a wing down to the bone. "Hey Cade," Ethan said with his mouth stuffed full.

"Where's your ma?" Cade asked.

Grabbing another wing Ethan pointed toward the kitchen.

"Better slow down there pal, leave some for the rest of us." He messed Ethan's hair one more time, heading for the kitchen.

Sarah looked tired, he thought. Her complexion pale and her eyes glazed filled with pain. She tossed the last of the red and white containers in the trash.

"Here let me," Cade offered, taking a platter of chicken from the counter.

"Thanks." She leaned back against the sink taking a deep breath.

"You okay?" he asked.

Sarah put on a week smile. "It's been a long day for all of us." She pushed back a wisp of hair tickling her cheek.

"Why don't you sit down? I'll take care of this." Cade walked inside the dining room and set the platter down on the table. He pulled out a chair for Sarah.

"This is probably a bad time to bring up this afternoon."

"Jenny means well." Sarah rubbed her temples. "She has her heart in the right place."

Cade picked up a piece of chicken. The sight and smell made his mouth water. "The horse, Apple." Cade didn't have a place for much in his life. He carried what he needed in his pack. The people in his life never stayed around him long. He didn't need them. He didn't need a horse, either. Yet, he asked anyway. "I want to adopt him."

Sarah looked upon him with curiosity in her eyes. "Is that what you and Jenny were arguing about?"

"I reckon you can say it was."

"You shouldn't argue with Aunt Jenny, you won't ever win," Ethan said.

"I reckon you're right about that too." Cade grinned at Ethan, who grinned back and reached for another piece of chicken.

Sarah grabbed a bowl of mashed potatoes and started forking some onto Ethan's plate. "Mom ..."

"You have to eat something else besides chicken," she said to Ethan.

"Apple's not adoptable. You've said it yourself." Sarah sat back down into her chair by Ethan. "Or is he?"

"No, he's still got a ways to go when it comes to manners." Cade piled his plate full of chicken.

"You want him?"

"Yeah, I do," Cade reached for the potatoes next.

"Momma says that sometimes you can't have what you want," Ethan said.

Cade chuckled. "That's a smart kid you've got."

Sarah smiled. She checked her watch and he knew she was waiting for Michael. Jenny would show up any minute too, and so he pressed on. "I can wait until you're ready to give him up, but no one else can adopt him, and I'd prefer he remained a stud."

"I think it would be great to have you adopt Apple, Cade. However, you would have to fill out an application like anyone else and part of that application states that you have a permanent address and a sufficient shelter."

"He couldn't stay here with your horses while I'm here?"

"I'm not saying that. It's just that Michael and I keep our horses in a private section of the barn. But what happens when you leave? You can't adopt Apple without having a home for him beyond Silver Wind."

"Trying to talk me out of it, are you?"

"Jenny seems to think you're a drifter." Sarah said.

"And you?"

The front door squeaked, Ethan jumped up, and dashed from the table.

Sarah tried wiggling out of her chair and Cade got up and helped her stand. "I think God brought you here for a reason. Where you go from here is between you and God."

Cade finished with his supper and slipped out while the small family sat and talked around the table. He'd tossed chicken and all the helpings on a plate. He walked over to Jenny's place and rapped on the door twice, but she didn't answer.

Cade noticed the for sale sign at the end of the lane. He hoped Mr. Zimmerman hadn't left yet to live with his son. He parked near the house and got out of the truck. As he approached the crooked front porch steps he heard noise from inside a nearby shed.

The shed door was flung wide open, and Mr. Zimmerman stood, hunched, over an old International truck.

"Howdy," Mr. Zimmerman said, and frowned as Cade stepped closer. "You're that fellow from the rescue."

Cade nodded, "I was hoping you'd remember me."

"Find a good home for Sheldon?"

"No, and that's kind of why I came by," Cade said.

Mr. Zimmerman laid down a wrench on the truck's motor and stared at him. His eyes were watery and sunken in his leather worn face. "Been off his oats lately?"

Cade nodded.

"I can't say I blame him. Gonna miss this place myself come a few days."

"So you've sold the place?" Cade asked.

"Nah, not yet. But I'll be moving on just the same." Mr. Zimmerman traded his wrench for a screw driver in the tool box at the bed of truck. Cade watched as he walked around and sorted through the tools.

"Need some help?" Cade offered. He hadn't seen an old truck like this since he was a teenager. His father had one just like it, before they sold it to his mother's brother to pay the farm taxes. He'd learned to drive in that old truck. He ran his hand over the dull orange paint of Mr. Zimmerman's truck.

"Just tinkering. Turns off on me from time to time. A few squirrels nesting in the engine didn't help none, not that I've taken it off the farm in a few years."

"Still, if you want a hand getting it running," Cade said.

"Was thinking I'd take her out one more time, you know, for old time sake." Mr. Zimmerman looked out toward the house and sighed.

"I'm sorry, it must be hard for you leaving your home and all."

Mr. Zimmerman shook his head and looked back at Cade. "There's no denying I'll miss this place, but I'm a long way from home. I'll get there soon enough though, soon enough ..." his voice trailed off.

Cade frowned. He glanced under the hood of the truck. Straw and grease, and frayed wires, it all made his gut twist. What did Mr. Zimmerman mean that he wasn't home yet? Did the old man really look that forward to dying? Or was he looking yonder to a new home as Cade once had when he'd ran off and eloped with

Crystal?

"You just drizzle some molasses in his oats, and ole Sheldon will come around. My missus always liked to spoil him that way, she did."

Cade tried to smile, but there was nothing happy about his thoughts or this old truck that wouldn't run.

"I think you've got it wired wrong," Cade said.

Mr. Zimmerman scratched his chin. "Know a thing or two about mechanics do you?"

"My dad had one of these when I was a kid. 1965 I think. Used to help him fix it now and then."

Mr. Zimmerman held out his screwdriver. "Then by all means, have at it."

Cade slipped off his long sleeve flannel shirt and hung it over the side view mirror. He took the screwdriver and leaned in alongside Mr. Zimmerman for most of the morning.

At lunchtime, he drained several glasses of lemonade and a few bologna sandwiches sitting on the porch. Mr. Zimmerman collapsed into a wooden rocker, and the swing beside it remained empty. A tattered blanket hung over the back and a hand embroidered pillow lay against one of the arm rests.

A gentle breeze cooled the sweat from his neck and the swing moved forward in the same rocking motion as Mr. Zimmerman's chair. He smiled, tilting back his head and closing his eyes.

Not long after, Cade suspected he'd fallen fast asleep. He would have pulled the blanket from the swing if he would have figured Mr. Zimmerman would not get offended. A real man never lets himself show weakness, Cade's father would have said that.

Cade left Mr. Zimmerman on the porch and headed back to the shed. He realized then that the dog on the porch the day before wasn't there. He looked back and frowned. What else had this man lost?

He glanced at the sodden clouds that shifted across the sky as if the hand of God pushed them aside. Where did he fall into all this, he wondered.

He stared at the front of the International truck with its hood up and its inner parts exposed. He wiped his mouth with his hand then grabbed his shirt. He figured he'd run into town, grab a few parts, and be back by the time the old man woke up again.

He didn't know why, but as he walked to Silver Wind's truck and opened the door, he felt a slight pang in his heart. It was almost as if he didn't want to leave. But he was coming right back, he shook his head.

As he drove back down the lane, he stopped, letting the truck idle as he stared at the for sale sign. It was then he decided he wasn't going anywhere—anytime soon.

CHAPTER 28

"Come on boy, it's time you and I took a ride."

Jenny cinched the girth of Clyde's saddle. Satisfied with the buckle, she rested her head against the English saddle's stirrup leathers. She took a deep breath, backed away from the saddle, and led the big black gelding to the mounting block.

Clyde sidestepped around and she had to turn him in a circle before he stood in the right spot for her to climb onto the block. He nickered and looked back at her. His ears forward attuned to her every word. "Why is it that all males have to be so difficult?"

Clyde murmured low in his throat in response. She felt the vibration as she pressed her hand to the side of his neck to steady him as she slipped her feet into the stirrups. Clyde danced and Jenny gave a small tug on the reins. He shook his head.

"Figures you would be difficult too," She gathered her reins and gave Clyde a small nudge. He took off in a canter, and Jenny lifted herself slightly off the saddle and went along for the ride with him. Giving him full rein, she and the black gelding raced across the open fields of Silver Wind at a neck breaking speed.

Clyde belonged to Michael, but ever since Sarah had grown more and more with child, poor Clyde had gotten rode less and less. Michael wouldn't mind, she was doing both him and Clyde a favor. Boy, did it feel good.

She laughed as Clyde darted to the right and headed for the hill behind the house. It would be dark soon, but she didn't care. It was just her, the horse, and God. She tightened her knees and took up a bit of Clyde's thick mane in her hands and let the wind hit her face.

She hadn't ridden in a few years, not since before collage, and her inner thighs ached with the effort to hold her seat. She pulled back on the reins, but Clyde chopped at the bit and pushed his nose forward. She tugged again harder, but Clyde raced faster.

Her heart seemed to match his frantic gait and Jenny leaned back and tried to regain her seat. Clyde slowed from his neck-breaking pace into a fast trot, the sudden abruptness jilted her. Jenny's foot slipped from the stirrups. She should have known better than to borrow Sarah's saddle and not adjust the stirrups to her length.

They were almost to the top of the hill. "Whoa boy ... Whoa ...." Clyde leaped into a run. Jenny tugged again to slow Clyde down. She sat deeper in the saddle and leaned back with all her strength, but Clyde jerked his head and fought against her tight hold on the reins.

At the top of the hill a cluster of low branch trees blurred before her. Jenny screamed and ducked. The reins fell loose against Clyde's neck and she clung to his mane for support. He sped up and Jenny slipped to the side.

With what little leather she held, she yanked back on the reins with one swift tug. Clyde reared and spun around. Jenny lost her seat and fell.

Pain exploded in her back as she hit the ground and she fought to breathe. Tears beaded in her eyes and every new attempt at breath hurt more than the last. She couldn't move, couldn't breathe, and curled herself up in a ball.

It came like spasms, small quick puffs of fresh air to her lungs, each one causing her throat to dry and her eyes to tear more. She stared up at the branches of a tree, blurred in her vision. If only she could reach one.

She flipped on her side, gasping for breath. Just when she thought she would never breathe again, her chest released and slowly her breathing came steady. She felt a warm nudge at her back. "Go away, this is all your fault," she cried.

"You know, one of these days you're going to have to stop doing that."

Jenny gasped; she looked over her shoulder at Cade. His was frowning with deep creases in his brow looking down at her.

"What are you doing here?"

"We'll get to that, but for now I need to know you're okay," he said.

She caught a glimpse of black behind him and soft brown eyes with a mussed forelock peek around his side. She glowered at the gelding. "I'm fine. Just fine."

She tried to get up and winced. Cade took her by the arm. "Just sit still for a minute. Anything broken?"

"Just my pride."

Cade chuckled, "Well, in that case let's get you to your feet then." He took her by the arm and pulled her up. She grabbed onto him, leaning on his strength to hold her. She didn't let go. She stood staring down at his flannel covered arms and took a deep breath. It hurt, but not half as much as it had before Cade had come.

He had the kind of arms that could wrap around a girl and make everything better. The kind that would never let go ... What was she thinking? Men like Cade didn't hold onto things, did they? Would he?

Jenny shook her head and let go. This was pure nonsense. How could she look at Cade and think that he was any type of husband material. She gasped, covering her mouth with her hand.

"Are you sure you're okay?" Cade asked.

Jenny stared at him. His eyes filled with concern. That's all it was, she told herself. Cade was concerned about her. He didn't love her—not like Brad had.

She shook her head again. She had to stop thinking like that. Brad was gone. He had a wife and a family. And she had … she had Cade.

How could she even consider falling in love with Cade?

"Can you ride, or would you rather walk? It's a bit far."

Jenny looked down from the hill and spotted the roof of the old farm house and the dotted fence posts of the corral illuminated by the descending sun.

She took one look at the black gelding snipping at grass behind Cade and sighed. "I think I'll walk."

"I figured you would. Besides, after the way this guy's been run, it'll do him good to cool down before we get to the barn."

It was then she noticed the wet rings on his sides and the sweat dripping down over his rump. Her heart softened and she walked over to Clyde. The black gelding backed up from her, and Jenny stuck her hands on her hips. "So that's the way you want to be after you went and dumped me."

Cade walked over and grabbed Clyde's bridle. "I would think you would want to thank him."

"Thank him?"

"Well, if it wasn't for seeing him racing down off the hill without a rider I wouldn't have known where to find you."

Jenny rubbed a sore spot on her back, "If it hadn't been for him, I wouldn't have been tossed flat on my back."

Cade grinned, "Got the wind knocked out of you, did ya?"

"It isn't funny."

Cade attempted to make a straight face, but his twinkling eyes gave him away. Jenny made a sound deep in her throat and began walking down the hill.

"Perhaps next time you'll keep a tighter rein."

"Next time? Who says there will be a next time?"

"You don't seem like the type that gives up easily." Cade fell in step beside her with the gelding following behind.

"What did you think you were doing out here alone anyway?"

Cade asked.

Jenny wrapped her arms around her waist as she walked. "That's none of your business, Cowboy."

Cade's eyebrow shot up. "They hang people for stealing horses you know."

She smiled. "Only in westerns." It made her think of the ones she sat and watched with her dad as a kid.

"Only a fool goes out riding and doesn't tell anybody they're gone. You missed supper." He leaned into her as she stumbled and she found herself grabbing onto his arm.

"If you want to get on and ride, I'll lead him," Cade offered.

Jenny looked back at Clyde. The black gelding's ears perked up at the mention of a ride. "No thanks."

"And women always say men are the most difficult."

"My father says it is because I'm a red head."

They walked the far distance back to the stables by the clinic where Bonnie, Sarah's beloved Thoroughbred mare, waited eagerly for Clyde's return. Together they gave Clyde a good rub down and an extra helping of oats before settling him back into his stall beside Bonnie.

"Quite a pair," Cade said.

"Yeah, who would have known."

Outside the golden hues of the late evening were washed with the darkening twilight. Cade walked Jenny to the stairs leading up to the second story apartment where she lived above the clinic.

She didn't seem to notice Cade's limp anymore—just his eyes and his smile. Goosebumps prickled down her arms and she rubbed them through her long sleeved shirt.

At the door, she pulled out her key from a string around her neck and unlocked it. She opened the door and looked back over her shoulder at Cade. "Well ...um ... goodnight."

"Aren't you forgetting something?"

She grabbed the doorknob until her knuckles turned white. Cade leaned in closer. His breath felt hot against her cheek. She closed her eyes. Her own breath hitched in her throat. Against her ear he whispered, "You're welcome."

CHAPTER 29

When Cade had finished dotting his i's and crossing his t's on the adoption application for Apple, he slid it towards Sarah along with a check for the adoption fee.

"The address won't take into effect for forty-five days, but I don't figure Apple will be ready to leave before then so it shouldn't matter."

Sarah scanned down over the application. She grimaced.

"Is everything all right? You did say I needed a more permanent address, right?"

Sarah looked up at him, a weary smile on her face, "Everything is good. You know you didn't have to go buy a place to adopt Apple. Although, I'm glad you've decided to stay nearby and continue to work here at Silver Wind."

"It's not every day you come across a place that feels like home," Cade said.

"If you don't mind me prying, but there are many of us who have wondered where home is for you." Sarah laid down the application on her desk. She grimaced again and shifted in her seat. Cade worried the humidity was making her uncomfortable in her condition. He glanced around spotting the window and walked over to turn on the air condition for her.

"I've got family in Texas. I suppose up till now, that's where you can say home has always been." Satisfied with the hum of the air conditioner kicking on, he turned back toward Sarah.

"Being on the road all the time must be exhausting." Sarah covered her mouth with her hand as she yawned.

It is what has kept him moving forward all this time. Getting hit by a truck had made him stop and look back at life. He needed it as much as he was sure he needed Apple and Silver Wind in his life—including Jenny.

He promised Mr. Zimmerman he would come by today, but he felt torn about leaving Sarah in her flushed and peaked condition.

"I can finish up here if you'd like to go back to the house where it is cooler," Cade said.

"Isn't Michael dropping you off at the Zimmerman place this morning?" Sarah asked.

"I can catch a ride later if you need help here."

Sarah leaned back in her chair and glanced around her. "There isn't anything here that can't wait till a little later. There won't be many more days when I get the chance to have some time to myself before the baby comes," she said more to herself than Cade.

He held out his hand to her, "You would be wise to take advantage of it." And he wasn't sure how much longer the sputtering air conditioner would keep up in this heat. They had an entire month to go until August came to an end. By the looks of Sarah, he feared the pregnant woman would melt before long.

"I could use a nap. It's becoming harder to get a good night's rest these days."

Cade was having some sleeping troubles of his own these days with the issue of Josh and Jenny on his mind.

"If you could check on the ponies before you go. I was thinking they could stay out all day in the lower pasture and we can bring in the yearlings. Michael needs to check the paint with the swollen knee when he gets back."

"Done," Cade smiled.

"I'll be in the house if anyone is looking for me," Sarah said.

Cade helped Sarah out of the chair and walked with her to the barn door. He watched her waddle her way to the house. Michael Wolfe was a lucky man to have a wife and family like Sarah and Ethan.

It made him think about the past and the future all at the same time. This time, however, he held no regrets. He looked out beyond Silver Wind and for the first time in years found peace with what tomorrow would bring.

Mrs. Miller had shown up at the clinic mid-morning and after pulling the files for Doc's appointments, Jenny headed over to the rescue. She tried calling Josh, twice, to get no answer.

She wiped the sweat from her brow as she entered the stables. Inside, it wasn't much cooler than out in the sun.

Today was her day off, and by the looks of things here at the stables, she doubted she'd make it to the ladies' Bible Study this evening, let alone finish those last few chapter questions she'd been struggling to answer.

She glanced inside the office to check on Sarah, but found Cade instead. "What are you doing in the office?"

"Same as you."

"I was looking for Sarah," Jenny said, feeling irate all of a sudden.

"She just left for the house. It's a might stuffy in here," Cade said.

Jenny sighed. "I suppose this heat is getting hard on her."

"Seemed a little tired, think she went up to the house for a nap. I told her I would help take care of things here so she could."

Jenny bit her lip. She was about to tell Cade they didn't need his help, but with Josh M.I.A. again, Ethan was with Michael in the clinic preparing to go out on calls this afternoon, that left only her and Cade.

"Good. More hands make less work. All the stalls need cleaned and make sure you mark the chart on the stall door so we know when it was done. If there is a horse in the stall, it needs groomed and we spend about twenty minutes with each horse to give it some attention."

"Isn't that Josh's duty?" Cade asked.

"Yes, but as you can see Josh isn't here," Jenny said.

"Out hauling is he?" By the look in Cade's eye, he knew Josh wasn't.

Jenny tilted her chin up a notch, "I'm sure he'll be here soon."

"Then he should be able to help you clean all these stalls. I've got horses to turn out and rations to check before heading over to the clinic."

Jenny planted her hands on her jean clad hips and watched him limp away.

Maybe if she would have been a bit more tactful with him she wouldn't have to grab a pitch fork and muck out all these stalls on her own.

Where was Josh? Lord, please don't let that brother of mine be getting himself into any more trouble.

They worked in silence. Cade took turns leading several of the horses out to pasture and brought a few in. He groomed the ones he handled, and he brought her a cold drink from the refrigerator in the office before he left for the clinic.

As the sun darkened and turned into a fiery globe of orange, Jenny heard a truck pull up alongside the stables. Soon she spotted Josh getting out of his truck. "Where have you been? You're supposed to be helping here at the rescue!"

Josh appeared taken back. "I picked up two horses for the clinic, Jenny. That's what I do."

"And it took you all day? I called twice. Where is your phone?" Jenny leaned against the pitch fork still in her hand.

"It does when I have to go across the state to get them!" Josh raised his voice back at her.

"And you couldn't return my call and tell me?"

"I don't have to answer to you, and even if I did, my phone isn't working right now." Josh brushed past her and headed inside the office.

Jenny leaned her pitch fork against the wall and followed him. "You're the foreman Josh. You can't leave Sarah and just run off and not have a way for anyone to get a hold of you. What happened to your phone? Did you break it?"

"It's called not paying the bill," Josh said.

"It's called not being responsible. I can't lend you anymore money. You already owe a month's salary," Jenny said.

Josh opened the small refrigerator on the far side of the office and scanned its contents.

"I *am* being responsible. Why do you think I went across the state today to haul a couple of horses?" Josh grabbed a soda and flicked it open.

"Great, but when you're not hauling there are stalls to clean and horses that need groomed and ..."

Josh held up his hand to stop her from going on while he guzzled down the soda. When he was finished he wiped his mouth with the back of his hand and crushed the can. "This was Sarah's idea, remember?"

"And we agreed to help her," Jenny said.

"No, *you* agreed we would help her. *Remember?*" Josh tossed the can in the trash and walked past her.

Jenny followed him back out of the office. "One of these days you're going to have to get over the fact she married Michael and not you."

Josh paused, turned on his heel and stared hard at her. Jenny stared back. She could see the conflicting emotions in her brother's eyes and deep down she'd hit a nerve in him.

Josh lifted his faded ball cap and repositioned it on his head. "I told you I'd help out when I can. I don't see you over here in the stables all the time, either."

"I didn't get these sitting at my desk at the clinic." She held out her blistered hands for him to see.

"And I don't get paid unless I haul something," Josh said.

"You'd get paid by the rescue if you'd ever show up," Jenny said.

"Not enough," Josh turned away and headed toward his truck.

"You already have free room and board, what else do you need?" she asked.

Josh waved her off, "I've got to go."

"Wait. Come back here. This conversation isn't finished."

"Then you finish it. I don't have time for a lecture, littler sister."

"I'm older." Jenny marched after him.

"A few minutes doesn't matter." Josh said.

"Where are you going, now?"

"Auction tonight, maybe I can pick up some business." Josh paused at his truck. His hand poised on the door handle. "A man's got to make his own way."

Now he sounded a lot like their father, Jenny thought, as she watched him get in the truck. Several papers and pieces of trash fell out as Josh slammed the truck door shut.

She watched him pull away and disappear down Silver Wind's lane.

She picked up the fallen papers and trash intent on tossing the in the garbage can until she noticed a ticket from a local race track. Her heart skipped a beat. *Oh Josh, what kind of trouble have you gotten yourself into?*

CHAPTER 30

Cade patted the Morgan on the neck and placed her back in her stall for the morning. As good as he felt, his ribs still throbbed with soreness reminding him to ease up on working so much. Michael and Sarah had told him to take it slow, any help here at the rescue was better than none.

He made sure the latch was closed on the stall door and moved over toward Apple. "Sorry, Pal. As muddy as the corral is with all the rain today, I think it best you stay inside today."

The stallion blew hard through his nostrils and Cade pulled an apple out his pocket he grabbed from the kitchen before coming to the barn this morning.

He would have to thank Jenny for stocking the refrigerator and cleaning up the house over the past few days.

Apple pressed his nose out through the stall door bars and snatched the fruit from Cade's hand. "You could have waited." He reached in and Apple allowed him to run his hand down the horses face for a moment before stepping out of reach.

Tomorrow, Cade decided, he would try Apple on a lead. Normally, he would have made faster progress with a horse like Apple, but his injuries had forced him to take it slow. He had a feeling his lingering presence around Silver Wind caused some upset with Jenny.

He chuckled.

After all, how could she help him and feel good about herself when he moved on if he stayed?

As Cade heard someone come into the aisle, he shook his head. "Just wait till she finds out I'm not going far," he told Apple.

He limped toward the office, hearing sounds of drawers slamming, Cade peered around the doorway. Josh hurried out the doorway, not giving Cade a second glance. He wondered if the other man had even noticed him standing there. About to call out to Josh, he clamped his jaw shut, thinking the better of it. Where ever Josh was headed, he was in a hurry.

Sheldon, the large workhorse, pounded on a stall door across from Cade. Seeing the lonesome horse, Cade said, "I'm all out of carrots, fellow."

Later, Cade found Mr. Zimmerman back inside the old man's barn with the hood propped up on the old International truck again. "Still not running right?"

Mr. Zimmerman looked over from having his head down near the engine. "Oh them parts got her running real good. New spark plugs." He held one up for Cade to see.

"Need some help?" Cade asked.

"Anxious to move in the place are you?" Mr. Zimmerman stepped back and shut the hood on the truck.

"Not much you can do in this rain," Cade said.

It had been raining since last night and Silver Wind didn't have an indoor arena to work with the horses. This surprised him, but there wasn't much he could do out in a muddy ring even with the rain cooling things down on this humid day. Perhaps he'd suggest to the Wolfe family about building in the outdoor corral and creating a new one on the side of the barn for time like these. He figured money was tight, but was sure with a little help they could come up with a way to expand the barn for an indoor arena.

With Sarah's blessing and use of her car, he'd set out to find a new ride of his own and found himself stopping in to check on Mr. Zimmerman.

"Sheldon all right? He perked up when you sweetened his feed, didn't he?" Mr. Zimmerman asked, concern deepening the wrinkles in his brow.

"Sure did." Cade didn't have the heart to share with Mr. Zimmerman that Sheldon would soon receive a new home. At the last open house, a woman had fallen in love with him. Cade wasn't sure what she loved more, the big blocky workhorse or the fact he was harness broken to pull her buggy at the next Harvest Parade.

He could see the grief in Mr. Zimmerman's eyes and didn't want to add to the old man's sorrow. It was tough enough losing a wife, and now to move from a place the man and his wife had called home all their lives.

Cade hoped one day he will feel the same way about this place. Home—an old farm house, a barn full of horses, and then an image of Jenny stepping off the front porch to greet him caused him to shake his head.

The rain pelted against the metal barn roof. It sounded like thousands of rocks pinging off the metal. Above them, at the roof pitch a steady stream of water dripped onto a pallet of seed corn.

"Help me cover that, will you?" Mr. Zimmerman made his way over to the sacks of corn. "I've been meaning to return these, unless you want it, little late to plant it this year, though."

"Can toss them on the back of the truck for you if you'd like, then you can take them into town when the rain stops."

Mr. Zimmerman waved his hand, "Sure. If you're willing to do that, I'd appreciate it."

Cade walked over and hefted up the first sack and tossed it onto the back of the truck. Mr. Zimmerman cleaned up his tools and put them in his tool box at the front of the truck.

Outside the wind picked up with the rain and lifted several tarps. Cade grabbed another sack of seed corn, spotting the vintage motorcycle under the flapping tarp. He whistled and plunked the bag of seed down on the bed of the truck.

Mr. Zimmerman walked out around as Cade went over and uncovered the motorcycle. "1969 Honda CB500 Sandcast. Took the missus around on it a time or two. Forgot it was still in here."

Cade took it by the handle bars and leaned over it. "Any chance it runs?"

"Don't know," Mr. Zimmerman said. "You're welcome to give it a try. One more thing I'm going to have to clear out of here before I hand this place over to you."

Cade ran his hand down over the leather seat. It was still in good shape for sitting out in the barn all this time. It was layered with dust and grime despite the tarp, and he rubbed his hand over the gold stripe on the gas tank.

"How long have you had it?" Cade felt like a kid at Christmas.

"I don't know, early 70's. Thought my boy would take an interest, but it was always cars with him."

Cade reached down and found the key in the ignition. He slid onto the bike, leaned down, and turned the key. It clicked as he figured it would.

"Got a battery charger around here somewhere," Mr. Zimmerman said.

Cade left the motorcycle sit where it was while he finished loading the seed corn on the back of the truck. Mr. Zimmerman found a battery charger, but Cade didn't think it would hold a charge so he took the battery off and put it on the back of the truck with the seed corn.

He and Mr. Zimmerman drove into town. It continued to rain, but Cade found he liked the old man's company. He listened to Mr. Zimmerman recount his days of building pieces onto the barn and updating the house. He could hear in the old man's voice the love and admiration he held for his deceased wife. It caused Cade to think about his own. He didn't know the plans God had for him, but he was certain this was the place God had chosen for him and for now that was enough.

When they returned to Zimmerman's farm, Cade placed the new battery on the motorcycle. The motorcycle groaned and clicked, but didn't start.

"Might need to check the fluids," Mr. Zimmerman said.

"You wouldn't want to sell it would you?" Cade asked.

"You get it to run and it's yours," Mr. Zimmerman told him.

"How much you want for it?" Cade wasn't used to anyone giving him anything.

"Keep your money. You'll need it to keep up with this old place." Mr. Zimmerman headed for the house in the sprinkling rain.

Cade spotted the mangy dog on the porch by the rocker as he felt a vibration on his hip. Grabbing his cell phone, he answered, "Hello."

CHAPTER 31

Jenny sat waiting by the door of the fourth floor hospital lounge. Her head buried in her hands, she took a deep breath and felt a tremble run down her spin to her toes.

Down the hall she heard boot clicks on the tile floor and looked up. Cade sat down beside her. He slipped a black Bible between her chin and lap. "I thought you might need this."

In her haste to find Michael, she had called Cade. Mrs. Miller had come to cover at the clinic and watch Ethan. Michael had arrived at the same time as the ambulance.

Jenny reached for the Bible and Cade's hand covered hers. She stared down at his hand. The Bible looked like the same one she'd held onto while she'd visited Cade in this very hospital. Ironic they should both end up back where they started, she thought.

Only now it was Sarah lying in a hospital bed instead of Cade, and unlike Cade, Sarah wasn't fighting for her own life, but for the life of her unborn child.

Cade leaned closer, pressing their shoulders together. He bent his head toward her, "Want to talk about it?"

"This would have never happened if Sarah would have listened to me." Jenny had lost count of the number of times she and Sarah had gone rounds about the stallion. No one she was certain had a deeper attachment to that horse than she did, but she'd learned a long time ago not to get attached to things for too long because someone else always needed them more.

She'd spent too many hours to count with that stallion. She'd poured her heart out to that horse on so many occasion and it hadn't done either of them a lick of good. She couldn't help wonder if Apple was abused and if his abuser was a woman.

She'd watched Cade working with him in the corral. She'd seen the way the stallion nuzzled up to him for an apple, and swiftly would turn the other cheek when Jenny approached.

'You can't save them all,' Josh had told Sarah as much on several cases. Jenny hadn't wanted to believe it in Apple's case, but here she couldn't turn away from the truth.

Apple was dangerous.

Michael should have gelded the stallion weeks ago. She had personally written the horse on the schedule twice and Michael scratched it off. Were they waiting for a time such as this?

Then there was Mr. Bailey's offer ....

"What happened?" Cade asked.

Jenny took a deep breath. This was as much as Cade's fault as it was hers, she decided. "Apple got out of his stall. Sarah found him running lose in the barn. He would have run Ethan down if Sarah hadn't stepped in front of him. Then Apple spun around and kicked at them." Her voice hitched, "She turned to shield Ethan and one of the horse's hooves nicked her in the side."

"Any idea how he got out?"

Jenny stared down at her hands. "You weren't around and Apple was getting restless, so I opened his stall door and tried to give him some extra hay. The door must not have latched the entire way."

Cade's nostrils flared and he kept a tight lip while he contemplated how to reply. Not that given the situation she wanted to argue with him anyway.

"You shouldn't have been messing with him alone. Where was

Josh?"

Jenny looked him right in the eye. "Obviously, the same place you were—nowhere to be found."

"I'm here aren't I? All you had to do was call," Cade didn't blink. He returned her stare.

She had no business asking, and Sarah would have asked the same thing. "Where were you?"

"Helping a friend," Cade said.

"A friend? I thought you were passing through these parts on your way to Augusta."

"Doesn't mean a man can't make friends."

"May I ask who this friend is?" Jenny asked.

"I was at the Zimmerman place."

"Mr. Zimmerman is your friend?"

"Not the only, I hope." Cade squeezed her hand.

A chill swept up her arms and she shivered.

"All right?" Cade asked.

Jenny bobbed her head, "I just got cold all of a sudden."

"It happens a lot in hospitals." Cade slipped off his jacket and wrapped it around her shoulders.

She listened as Cade told her about helping Mr. Zimmerman fix his truck and return the seed corn. "Sounds like you've been spending a lot of time over at the Zimmerman place."

"He gave me a 1969 Honda Sandcast, too."

Jenny didn't know what that was and it showed on her face because Cade grinned and said, "It's a motorcycle."

"A Honda?" Jenny gasped. "What happened to the Harley boy?"

Cade chuckled, "You can't beat vintage, which brings me back to where I was when you called."

Jenny's fingers felt ice cold. Poor Ethan had helped Sarah get into the office and called for help. Remembering the pain Sarah had been in when Jenny found her caused her chest to tighten and a new lump to form in her throat. She bent forward, forehead to forehead, leaning against Cade. She squeezed her eyes shut. Why couldn't it have been Josh who'd gone to the stables? Or Cade?

Apple had dragged Cade around a time or two and he hadn't ended up back in the hospital.

Why did it have to be Sarah? And the baby?

By the time the ambulance and Michael arrived, Sarah was having pains ripple across her abdomen. It was too early for the baby, yet. Jenny pulled away from Cade.

On her feet, she paced back and forth in the small waiting area. She laid the Bible down beside Cade. She glanced down the hall and sighed. Before Michael had come back into Sarah's life, it was always Jenny at Sarah's side. She was there for Ethan's birth, and now she waited by the sidelines feeling helpless.

And she didn't like this feeling, not one bit.

"It doesn't matter. What is done is done." Jenny turned away from him. She pressed her knuckles to her eyes to hold back the tears threatening. Any moment, Michael would come walking down the hall with news about Sarah, she hoped.

She pulled her phone from her jeans pocket and checked for any messages. With Ethan at the clinic with Mrs. Miller and Josh on the road to who-knows-where again, there was only one thing she could do—wait.

Since Sarah wouldn't listen to her, Jenny had taken matters into her own hands.

Yet, the decision didn't bring any comfort, not like having Cade here with her. Funny, as much as she wanted to have him go, she wanted him to stay.

Cade stood beside her. Putting his arm around her, he pulled her into his embrace. She laid her cheek against his chest and closed her eyes, praying she had done the right thing.

Later in the evening, Cade walked through the barn. It had stopped raining, and the coolness of the barn was a welcomed retreat. Cade wasn't one for lingering around hospitals any longer than necessary.

Michael approached him in the hospital and asked him to take care of things back here at the clinic and rescue. Jenny insisted on coming along, but Michael had convinced her to stay and sit with Sarah a bit.

They'd given Sarah medication to stop the contractions and kept her comfortable to rest for the night.

After tending to the horses at the clinic and checking in with Doc Miller, Cade had headed to the rescue barn.

He found Apple back in his stall with a rope tied around the gate. Cade wiggled the broken latch. "This won't do now will it?"

Apple's ears perked at Cade's voice and the stallion spun around to face him.

"You caused quite a bit of trouble today," Cade told the horse.

Apple bobbed his head up and down. He pressed his nose against the bars on the door, the horse's upper lip jutting out. Cade took a step back. "No treat for you, Pal. You hurt Mrs. Wolfe and put her baby in danger."

The stallion pawed at the door.

"No wonder the latch is broken." Cade glanced at the rope tie. "At least that is one thing I can fix tonight."

Down the aisle Cade heard a door shut. He walked past the feed room, and around the corner he spotted someone going into the office.

Inside, he caught Josh with his hand on the upper left drawer of Sarah's desk and a wad of cash in the other.

"Tell me you're borrowing it," Cade said.

Josh's face turned as red as his hair. He glared at Cade for a long minute before putting the cash in the drawer and shutting it. "I'm returning it."

"Along with the money you've borrowed from everyone else around here?" Cade stood, blocking the doorway.

"Mostly." Josh's eyes narrowed on him. "Not that it is any business of yours."

"Since I've been helping out around here, I'd say it's my

business."

Josh strolled around the desk and smirked. "Helping out around here or taking advantage of my sister?"

Cade held up his hand. "I'm no one's charity case and that money you have there is for the care of these horses, not whatever financial troubles you've caused yourself of recent."

He felt a soft spot for the younger man standing in front of him.

"Who says I'm in any kind of trouble?" Josh hooked his thumbs in his belt loops. He was much like his sister, Cade thought, neither one of them would ever admit it, either.

"Call it a hunch." Cade shrugged. He saw some of himself in Josh and it was a shame to see some struggling to find their feet without someone to help hold them steady.

"I wouldn't bet on that if I were you. You may lose," Josh walked toward him. "Now, if you'll get out my way I need to get going before I'm late."

"There's no place that important that you have to rush off without taking care of your responsibilities."

Josh bumped into Cade, trying to push him aside. Cade shoved him back.

"You're in no position to tell me what to do."

"Sarah's in the hospital," Cade held his stance.

Josh staggered back a step or two. Quick to recover from the news, he said, "So?"

Cade shoved as Josh pushed him. "She got hurt because she was trying to do your job."

Cade tried to read Josh's expression, but the younger held his poker face. "Looks to me like you're doing a good job around here without me," Josh grunted.

"What will you do when there isn't anyone around to bail you out?"

"Jenny didn't figure you would stick around for long," Josh said.

"Her plan. Not mine."

"You'd be best to stick with it."

"Which? The one where I stay or the one where I go?" Cade asked.

Josh smirked. "Whichever one Jenny decides. If you haven't learned by now, she always knows what is best for everyone."

"I take it that includes twin brothers," Cade said.

"Two minutes older and wiser."

"Then you'd be wise to give me a hand around here before you take off. I hear there is no wrath like that of a woman scorned."

"Not tonight. Fortunately for me, I know how to deal with my sister. You on the other hand." Josh made a face. "You're on your own."

Josh shoved his way past Cade.

"I can manage fine on my own." Cade said, thinking *until now.*

"You like her, don't you?" Josh glanced back over his shoulder. "Oh man, and you thought I was the one with troubles."

Cade could hear Josh laughing the whole way outside the barn.

CHAPTER 32

It was a little after ten that night when Jenny heard a truck pull up alongside the stables. She'd sat in Sarah's seat in the office staring down at the adoption form for almost two hours. That had been a long time to sit and think. A long time to wonder if she'd made the right decision by calling Mr. Bailey.

She sighed, hearing a truck door shut. The engine still rumbled and light shone into the stable's entrance from a set of headlights.

She pulled her sweater more securely around her and walked out into the stable's walkway to greet him.

Like most people adopting a horse, he'd been eager. So eager, he'd insisted on coming right away.

Cade hadn't been easily persuaded to leave the barn. He'd insisted on walking her home after he'd finished feeding the horses and repairing the broken latch on Apple's stall door.

Both Sarah and the baby were stable, but the doctor insisted she stay on bed rest now until the baby was born. The last thing she needed to see coming home was Apple. Jenny supposed, she too, would miss the unruly stallion.

She encountered Mr. Bailey's shadow stretching down the barn aisle that led her to him. He was a black figure against the beams of light in the night. "I know I'm doing the right thing," she whispered.

"I appreciate you waiting up for me," Bailey said. "I was afraid you might have second thoughts before I got here."

"Now why would I do that?" Jenny asked.

"You didn't sound too sure on the phone." He tilted his head looking past her. "No guard tonight?"

"Cade, you mean? He's probably fast asleep at the cottage house by now." What was she doing? She forced a smile, not that he would see it beyond the shadows of the head lights.

"Wise choice. You know, leaving him to sleep while we get down to business." Bailey stepped forward and Jenny stepped back.

"You can pull your trailer back against the doors here. I'll get some feed to lure him on. As I said on the phone, I'd like to do this as quickly and quietly as possible."

"I like your style. Perhaps when were done here ..."

"Let's just get this taken care of first," she said, her hand trembling as she pointed to the corral. "Then you can sign the papers here in the office."

Bailey tipped back his Stetson, "Strictly business. I like that about a woman. Alright, how about turning on some lights for a man to see what he's doing?"

"I'd rather not, unless you want to risk Cade seeing the lights and wondering what's going on this late at night." Why did it matter to her if Cade saw the lights?

Michael had taken Ethan to spend the night with a friend.

Sarah would understand, or at least Jenny prayed she would.

"Gonna be hard seeing in the dark, but I suppose if you help direct me, it might be possible. Don't know why we can't just lead him out of the stall and into the trailer." Bailey complained.

"I don't know ..." Jenny said. She'd seen Cade leading the horse around the corral a time or two. "I guess it wouldn't hurt to try."

"I'll move the trailer closer to the entrance if you turn on the back lights inside here, that way at least one of us can see what we're doing."

Jenny walked over near the far wall by the office door and flipped on the back lights of the stable. Several horses jerked their heads up, but none protested the soft glow of light coming from the walkway.

"That a girl." Bailey grinned.

"I'll grab a rope while you back up," Jenny said.

She watched as Bailey walked back to his truck and got in. As he maneuvered his truck, ready to back his trailer to the entrance door, she headed down the walkway.

"Oh Lord, I know this is the right thing to do. I just know it. But why doesn't it feel right?" she whispered. She walked to Apple's stall, grabbed the lead rope from beside the door, and stared into the shadows of the stallion's stall. Apple stood with his ears forward and his dark glassy eyes watching her.

"Why aren't you sleeping like the rest of the horses?"

Apple shook his head, sections of his mane flopping to the other side of his neck.

"What? No teeth? No kicking? Let's just hope you're too tired to protest, shall we?" Jenny took a deep breath and slid the latch of Apple's stall door free. She waited a heartbeat. Apple stood watching, his ears now pinned forward. "I suppose I should have brought you a treat. I'm sorry, fellow. I don't have any apples tonight."

Apple nickered in response. His stable mates shifted, some pressing their noses to the bars, others snorted softly in their slumber. Jenny sighed. "All I'm going to do is put this lead rope on you, okay? We're gonna walk up that aisle and get onto the trailer."

Apple lifted his head up and away from her reach. "Be a good boy, okay? No one is going to hurt you." *Not like the way you hurt Sarah.*

Jenny slid the stall door open, she cringed waiting for Apple to plow her over as he had almost done to Ethan and Sarah.

Apple backed into the corner of his stall. She heard the trailer rattle and glanced down the walkway to the entrance. A few more feet and Bailey would have the trailer parked, ready to go.

"Okay boy, I'm just going to put this lead rope on you." Her hands trembled, holding out the lead rope. Apple took another step back, scrunching himself into the corner. Jenny's arms quivered like rubber holding out the lead. "I'm just going to take you for a walk. Then you'll be off to your new home. Won't that be nice? You'll have someone to love you and care for you and who will work with you every day."

Didn't Cade already do that? Didn't Apple already have a home here at the rescue? And, didn't she love him?

Jenny took another deep breath, and stepped forward. She had to do this—for Sarah. She blinked, blinked away the tears building behind her lashes. Since when did she get all emotional over a horse?

How many times had this stallion tried to run someone down or cause harm? What if the next time it was Josh, or Cade?

Hadn't Apple dragged him through the barn, too?

Closing her eyes briefly, standing there holding out the lead, she prayed for strength. Opening her eyes again, she willed her hands to steady, her heart to stop its furious pounding and stepped into the stall with the stallion.

She didn't think, she didn't give herself the time or the privilege, afraid she'd back out again. She snapped the lead onto Apple's halter. Expecting him to rear or charge she stepped to the side, but Apple just looked at her. His hind quarters quivered.

"Now that wasn't so bad, was it?"

"Just hold up and I'll grab an extra rope and give you a hand," Bailey called.

Apple jumped, slamming her against the wall. Her shoulder hit the bars as her side grazed the corner feeder. She groaned, tears coming to her eyes. Apple held her hostage in the top corner of his stall.

She heard Bailey running down the walkway. "Whoa! Whoa!"

she cried, as Apple spun in the direction of Bailey.

"Stop!" she cried, slipping under the feeder and towards the open stall door before Apple escaped without her.

Apple reared back and ran into Bailey in the doorway. Bailey grabbed a hold of her and yanked her out of the stall. Apple snorted. He stood with the lead now dangling from his halter to the ground. He didn't move.

"I think I'll take it from here. We'll just chase him up into the trailer. I've got the doors closed. We'll herd him up in with a rope from behind."

Jenny rubbed her shoulder and glanced over at Apple.

"You alright?" Bailey asked.

Jenny nodded, she stared at Apple. Why did the stallion stand there and look at her like that? She must be tired, she decided, turning away from the horse. "I guess so."

"Stand back," Bailey said.

Jenny moved out of the way and Bailey slid the stall door the whole way open. Apple didn't move.

Bailey looked at Jenny, his eyebrows rose.

Jenny shook her head. "Go on, what are you waiting for?"

Still Apple stood, gazing back at her with his big glassy dark eyes that made her heart squeeze.

"I'll go in and shoo him out."

Jenny grabbed Bailey arm. "No, wait." She stepped in ahead of him. She reached out, slowly, and placed her hand on Apple's blaze. "I don't think he wants to go."

Bailey chuckled, "Now don't be going and changing your mind on me. I came a long way to come back here for this horse. Probably hasn't been out of his stall enough to know to walk through the doorway."

Jenny held her hand back, blocking Bailey entrance into Apple's stall. With her hand still on this blaze, she ran her other hand down the side of his face. "You can't stay here," she said.

Behind her Bailey made a sound in his throat.

She ignored him, softly running her hands down Apple's

blaze. As she reached for the lead rope Apple swung away, leaving her standing in front of his rump.

Bailey yanked her out of the stall. "I don't have all night." He walked in, grabbed the lead, and tugged on it. Apple swung his head around and Bailey backed out of the stall. Jenny ran to the feed room and grabbed a can of oats.

She shook it, and several horses shifted in their stalls. She heard Apple squeal and the stallion charged out of his stall knocking Bailey down. Jenny bit her lip, shaking the can and as Apple ran straight towards her she tossed the oats onto the floor of the trailer. Apple galloped past her and jumped into the trailer.

Not far behind him, Bailey jogged up and slammed the trailer door shut. Apple rammed the side of the trailer, and as he kicked the door, Bailey pulled down the lever on the trailer gate and grinned. "Now that wasn't as bad as I figured."

Jenny leaned back against the cold steel gate of the trailer and breathed. *No, it had been worse.*

Inside the trailer, Apple continued to ram the sides and kick. The stallion reached his muzzle out the uncovered side slots and bared his teeth.

"I believe you've got some papers for me to sign?" Bailey said, pulling her out of her stupor.

She moved away from the trailer, "They're here in the office." He held out his hand for her to go first. She glanced back over her shoulder at the trailer. Apple stared back at her through the open slots of the back trailer gate. His eyes no longer shone glassy, but wide with fright. A trickle of blood ran down one nostril from where he'd bumped his muzzle against the trailer.

Jenny stepped into the office. She picked up the papers on the desk. Bailey pulled a pen out of his pocket. As he signed the adoption papers, Jenny hugged herself.

When Bailey was finished, she forced herself to smile. She separated the papers and handed him the yellow carbon copy. "And before I forget," he said, pulling a wad of bills from his back pocket. "I believe this will cover the adoption fee."

He placed the bills on the desk beside the adoption papers. She didn't have to count to know that he'd made a sizable donation beyond the adoption fee. "Don't you worry about stopping in; I'll take good care of him."

Jenny nodded. Under normal circumstances she, Sarah, or Josh would stop in to check on the horse in its new home after a week or so. Perhaps, just this once, it wouldn't be necessary.

"Although, if you're ever at the rodeo, look me up. The offer still stands."

She walked him out into the walkway of the stables. She watched as he got into his truck and drove away. Apple stared out from the back.

"It's for the best," she said, turning back inside the stables and turning off the light.

CHAPTER 33

"It looks as if you've had a rough night." Mrs. Miller stood from Jenny's spot at the reception desk in the clinic. "I've got coffee brewing in the back, not decaf either. I figured you'd need something to help keep you strong this morning."

Jenny blinked. She barely slept hearing a little voice sing song in her head. B*ig mistake. Big mistake. Big mistake.*

To make matters worse, she couldn't seem to get warm this morning. Her finger tips and toes were ice cold and a shiver ran down her spine.

She hoped she wasn't coming down with anything. These past few days had cooled the air and left a dampness clinging to everything, including her chest. Every time she took a breath and thought of last night, it became harder to breath.

She'd done what she needed to do, but that didn't explain why Mrs. Miller was here. Nor why she was here so early. Unless …

"It's okay," Mrs. Miller said as she walked around the desk and led Jenny to get some hot coffee. "Michael picked up Ethan last night. They've stopped the contractions. Sarah has to keep still for the next month, but the baby's okay."

Jenny leaned back against the counter near the coffee pot. "I never want to have this happen again."

She didn't have the heart to tell Mrs. Miller she had received this same information, too.

"She's coming home later today. Michael said for us to re-schedule his appoints for today and Mr. Sheridan is tending to the horses in the clinic."

Cade was in the clinic barn? Did he know Apple was gone? She gripped the mug Mrs. Miller handed her and took a deep hot gulp of coffee, praying for it to calm her nerves. "Thanks for coming in and letting me know."

There was silence in the room.

Finally Mrs. Miller spoke up. "I almost forgot. Mr. Sheridan has requested you meet him over at the rescue barn first thing this morning."

Jenny let the warmth of the ceramic mug radiate heat to her cold fingers. "It'll have to wait, I need to make those phone calls and reschedule Michael's appointments today."

"I can take care of that. You've shown me enough on the computer. I'll manage fine here while you're gone." Mrs. Miller stepped out into the hallway as Doc approached. The married couple exchanged a glance as Doc Miller walked past them.

Jenny knew what they were thinking.

Her gut twisted and she set down her mug on the counter. Mrs. Miller laid her hand on Jenny's shoulder. "You needn't worry. I've watched the way you've taken care of this place. You place many burdens upon yourself for someone so young. Now you need to let someone else lend a hand while you, my dear, meet Mr. Sheridan at the barn. "

"I have a feeling this might take a while." Jenny was glad Mrs. Miller was here this morning. She didn't like to admit she needed help, but without Sarah able and Josh willing to fulfill their duties at the rescue she feared she was getting over her head.

"Take all the time you need," Mrs. Miller said.

Jenny slumped in relief. "I owe you one."

"We'll talk about that later." Mrs. Miller steered Jenny back down the hall. "If I were you, I wouldn't keep a handsome young gentleman like Mr. Sheridan waiting too long."

At the door, Jenny glanced back at Mrs. Miller and the older woman winked at her. Despite her chills, Jenny's face flushed with heat.

Outside the clinic she told herself it was time to stop thinking of the 'what if's' and start focusing on the here and now.

Which just circled her thoughts right back to Cade Sheridan.

For two months, *two months*, Cade had been working with that stallion. His suspicions had been confirmed this morning when he found Apple's stall empty. He checked every stall in the barn, outside the corral, and ridden Michael's black around the pastures to account for all the horses.

They were all there, except Apple.

His insides curled up thinking about Jenny and the situation he would have to face. He'd stopped trying to understand the ornery red head a while ago, but she was a firecracker. He never knew when she'd explode.

Of all the hot headed things she could have done!

But the fact she'd gone and given the stallion away …it cut deeper than Crystal's betrayal.

He paced inside Sarah's office. There was no time to wait any longer. Apple could have been trucked across the state by now and once the horse was unloaded there was no telling which rodeo circuit to search.

It had been over an hour since he left the clinic and asked Mrs. Miller to relay his message. Cade pounded a fist down on the desk.

Rather than stand around any longer, Cade grabbed the keys to Michael's truck and swung open the office door. Jenny stood wide-eyed in front of him. Her hand poised, reaching for the door handle.

"We have to talk. Now."

"You're upset about Apple," she said it in a slow calm voice. Her pale cheeks and blood shot eyes spoke of her guilty conscious. Good, he thought, about time she saw she wasn't always right.

"You've gotten yourself in a lot of trouble this time."

Jenny's expression was one without a care for what he said. "Look," she said, the green in her eyes swirling with a surprising vulnerability. "I get why you're upset. But Apples needs someone who can work with him for a long time and give him a good home and, well, you're only here until your next job. You saw what happened last night. When you leave, who knows what might happen with a horse like Apple in the barn. What if that was someone from one of our open houses opening the stall gate when no one looking? We can't have anyone else get hurt, let alone for the rescue to have a law suit on our hands."

His gaze slid down her battle-ready stance and back up to her face. "That wasn't your call to make."

"With Sarah in the hospital, I had every right to make that call."

Cade squeezed his fist around the truck keys tighter. "How so?"

"Because I can," Jenny snapped. "Sarah, Josh, and I ... we put this place together, and as such, I have the right to approve an adoption. Whether you like it or not, I'm in charge here."

Her eyes blazed and her chin lifted. If it wasn't for her, he wouldn't have come here in the first place.

But this wasn't about him. Or even Jenny.

This was about a young stallion, and had been from the moment he walked into the barn this morning. Because most horses were well cared for in the circuit, but Cade knew Bailey's employer was different.

His ex-father-in-law never cared about the horses as much as he did the business. Because a horse like Apple deserved a home with a pasture and place where he could run until his heart was content, Cade would have to retrieve him ... no matter the cost.

There was no turning back, and Jenny was going to listen to him. "Then if you're in charge, you would have known that Apple was adopted weeks ago," he said, knowing his eyes were flashing some hard steel in her direction.

"Sarah would never have approved of Bailey adopting Apple."

"She didn't."

"Then who?" Her long-lashed eyes narrowed to slits.

"Me."

"You," she scoffed. "You have to have a home—an address to adopt a horse. Sarah would never have approved, and even if she did, she would have told me."

"The paperwork is in the files in the desk. Go see for yourself," he snapped, reining in his frustration, fighting to remain level headed, and losing. They were wasting time.

Jenny plowed into the office and Cade stepped aside. She yanked open the file drawer and pulled the stallions folder. It was the first one in the drawer. Opening it knocked the wind from her sails. Her lips hung in an 'o'. "Th-this isn't right. The address is local."

"It's right. That's my address, and Apple belongs to me. Satisfied?"

"Well," she snapped, her glare steamy. "We shall see about this."

"You go ahead and do that. He reached over and took the papers from atop Sarah's desk.

"What are you doing? Those belong to the rescue," Jenny reached for them.

"And the horse belongs to me. I'm going to take back what belongs to me." His heart hurt at her expression. He'd regret for the rest of his life how his marriage had ended, but he knew no matter what he could have done, it wouldn't have made things different. God gave him a second chance coming here. He planned to do everything in his power not to waste it—starting by getting his horse back.

He walked out of the office and strode out to where he left the truck parked. Taking a deep breath, he prayed silently for God to give him a hand.

CHAPTER 34

"This is preposterous," Jenny declared slamming the car door shut. She rushed over to where Cade was hitching the trailer to the truck. "The address on that adoption paper was the Zimmerman farm."

"Yep."

"You want me to believe you bought the place?"

"Yep."

The combination of those unforgettable eyes, mop of sand-colored hair, and that chiseled jaw made her temperature rise. She had to be coming down with some kind of bug.

"And you can't tell me you didn't adopt Apple because of some personal thing you have going with Bailey that you won't tell me about?"

His gaze drilled into her, and she knew he could see through her shielded eyes to the troubled waters behind them. "Something like that."

"Then maybe I made the right decision and Apple is better off where he is."

Cade straightened. "Figured you lost sleep over it. Most people do when they know they've done something wrong."

"I admit I've had second thoughts about my decision. That

doesn't mean it was wrong."

"Get in and we'll go find out."

She got in and plunked herself down into the seat beside him. She scooted closer to the door.

"I thought rodeo cowboys were supposed to take good care of their horses," Jenny said.

"Most of them do." Cade said as they pulled out of the clinic driveway. Once they were on the road he pushed the adoption paper toward Jenny. "Punch the address in, will you?"

"Sure, but when we get there I'm sure we'll see Apple is fine." She tried to ignore the turbulent emotions swirling inside her.

"Let's hope you're right."

"You know, sometimes it's best if you confront someone who has hurt you in the past. Tell them how you feel and even forgive them."

Cade's knuckled turned white on the steering wheel. She didn't mean to cause the vein at the base of his neck to jump like that.

She remained quiet while he drove. Soon, he relaxed his hold and his shoulders slumped.

She would have almost believed the tension had released its hold on him, but then he said, "I did confront him ... with my fists."

Jenny gasped.

Cade glanced over at her when they came to a stop sign. "That surprises you?"

"No ... yes ..." She shook her head, confused. She'd had him pegged for a rough ridden low down cowboy when she first met him. Not many cowboys' rode motorcycles and not many of them rode up a hill to rescue her, either.

However, one thing she had come to learn about Cade was that he was honest. And, that whatever kind of man he had been before the accident, he was different now.

Cade grinned. "Can't ever seem to make up your mind, can you?"

"Yes, I can."

"Then which is it?" he asked.

"Which is what?"

Cade chuckled. "Just don't want to say it, do you? Go ahead; my hands are on the steering wheel."

She looked out at the trees and traffic passing by. Or maybe it was them passing by and the trees were standing still. It would be hard to go anywhere when you were rooted. Is that what kept Cade wondering? Did he not have any roots anyplace to hold him?

Jenny sighed. She looked across the seat at him. "I believe that who you were in the past isn't who you are now. But I also believe in forgiveness and letting ourselves heal through grief of losing that part of our lives."

Cade didn't reply. She took his silence as a cue the conversation would go no further.

She had been a good one to use those words, "forgiveness," and "loss". It wasn't like she'd ever lost someone as Cade or Sarah had lost a parent.

She also had Josh, as annoying as he maybe at times. He was still her twin brother.

Yet, she'd lost Brad and now Apple, both her decision. Maybe, but Brad really wasn't something she'd lost. She'd never really had him in the first place.

Before she could restrain herself, tears slipped from the corners of her eyes and slid down her cheeks.

She ducked her head away from Cade and hid her face in the bend of her arm.

"There are tissues in the glove box," he said.

Her face flushed and she looked away.

"It will take a few hours to get there. You can rest if you'd like." Cade reached over and took her hand. His touch took her by surprise. His warm fingers curled around her cold ones. His thumb rubbed gently over the top of her hand.

His actions baffled her. She wanted to explain to him her justifications for giving Apple to Bailey. She wanted to apologize for not knowing he adopted Apple, but she was angry at him for not telling her he bought the Zimmerman place.

It wasn't as if she had any claim on his life. She wanted to do the right thing. She wanted him to heal and continue on his way hoping by helping him it would bring closure for her.

She was wrong.

No matter how many times she told herself there could never be anything between them, she was having a hard time convincing her heart otherwise. There was no way she could feel anything for him other than responsibility—and friendship.

She had to keep thinking rationally. But she'd stopped all rational thinking last night when Cade wrapped her in his arms at the hospital. She put her free hand against her pounding temple. Her head was too crowded with her thoughts and emotions at war.

This little excursion to find Apple made her feel worse.

"Don't worry. We're not coming home without him."

If only he knew that's not what she'd been crying about.

Cade pulled to a halt in front of the abandoned camper. He checked the directions in his phone's GPS before glancing over at Jenny. She was sound asleep with her legs tucked and facing toward him.

There were no signs of Bailey or anyone else around the old camper. After contemplating whether to wake her up, Cade opened the truck door. Because he knew there was no one here, he didn't bother knocking on the camper's door. He strode through the tall grasses to the small barn on the other side of the dirt drive.

One door hung open a broken hinge and the other was nailed shut. Inside a plume of dust swirling in the air welcomed him. Slants of light shone through the missing boards in the back of the barn.

Suffocating weight settled over him, as if he had the whole world on his shoulders. While he had the stallion sitting on one shoulder, Jenny sat on the other. He had the impulse to back out of here and hit the open road again.

Back at the truck, Jenny leaned against the truck bed and rubbed her eyes.

"Are you all right?" Cade asked, standing close to her. He'd managed to get over his anger with her a few miles back.

"I'm fine," she said.

"Are you sure?" he asked. "You've been sleeping for almost three hours. I didn't want to wake you."

"Just tired," she peered around him. "Why are we here?"

Cade tensed, unsure how she would react. "This is it."

She stepped away from the truck and put her hands on her hips. He waited patiently for her to turn around again. "There's no one here, is there?" she asked, her voice calmer than he expected.

She covered her mouth with her hand and stared at him. For once, she appeared more like a frightened kitten than the spitfire he knew she was.

"The barn is empty. They're no tracks here, except ours. By the looks of things, I'd say no one's been here for some time."

"Where else could he be? This is the right address, isn't it?" She walked back towards the truck. He reached at the same time she did to open the truck door.

A smile wobbled across her lips. Their eyes met and gazes locked. There was something in that look that reached out and touched him. He slid his hand over hers. Like his heart pounding in his chest, her pulse raced wildly beneath his thumb.

"I suppose this is where you tell me, 'I told you so.'"

Still holding her hand, he pulled her closer to him. Leaning close to her ear, he said, "Nope. You just did."

She gasped and shoved him away.

Cade laughed, pulling her closer to him. She didn't have a chance at escaping. He lowered his head and kissed her. He'd been waiting for this moment for the longest time, it seemed.

When he lifted his lips from hers she asked, "Where do we go from here?"

"How about we start at the rodeo?"

CHAPTER 35

It was a long shot. One he was willing to take if it meant finding the stallion.

After making a few calls, he redirected their route to the Kentucky State fairgrounds.

It had taken Cade years to acknowledge there was more to life than riding broncs. The rodeo world felt natural to him. Probably why he still was always moving on to the next ride, except leaving had been the hardest decision of his life.

Back then he had been surrounded by men who lived the same kind of life. They were all buddies, none of them real friends, because real friends didn't steal another man's wife.

After Jenny brought him to Silver Wind, Cade started wondering what it was like to have real friends, neighbors, and a place that didn't change with each new job. That's why he bought the Zimmerman place. He wasn't sure if he'd wear his welcome out, but he had to take the chance. Silver Wind and its people had grown on him.

It would make his mother happy to know he had chosen to settle down at last. She was always telling him he needed to find his place. Cade half-agreed with his mother; his rodeo days were gone and it was time to start living a regular life.

He looked over at Jenny at and found her standing in a group of cowboys, their faces showed their annoyance. He chuckled to himself. He couldn't leave her alone for one minute since they arrived at the rodeo without her stirring up trouble.

Cade should have left her there, knowing she was about to become blown off by those men.

One walked away, with a number on his back, no doubt heading for his chute.

He walked close enough to hear Jenny speak softly, but sternly to the other men. She could have been a detective for the CIA the way she fired question after question. Some things she asked about the horses and where they went, and sometimes she brought up Bailey.

The cowboys shook their heads and put their hats back on. He placed his hand on Jenny's shoulders.

He recognized Bart Hall and Jerry Reese. "Good to see you boys again."

They shook hands around Jenny.

"You know each other?" she asked, a hint of annoyance in her voice.

"Why I haven't seen you since Denver ….or was it Tuscan a few years back?" Bart asked.

"Can't say I'm surprised after what happened, but glad to see you're back." Jerry said.

"I'm just here trying to find my horse. A rowdy buckskin stallion, would have stepped out of a Double D trailer."

"Ah, so that's what the little lady has been trying to get out of us?" Jerry chuckled.

Bart scratched his head. "Must be the hair, I got confused. Could have sworn your missus was a long blond haired gal."

Cade put his arm around her waist and drew her near. He imagined sliding his hand through the smooth locks of her hair and then dipping her head back a little so he could—

Jenny opened her mouth to speak, but Cade interrupted. "Any idea where we can find him?"

He needed to stay focused on finding Apple and save those other thoughts for another time.

"I guess you hadn't heard. Double D no longer has the contract here. Heard tell old Dale's been keeping his business close to home lately." Jerry shifted his feet and glanced over his shoulder.

Jenny turned toward him. "So Apple's at the Double D? Maybe Mr. Bailey really is going to take care of him like he said he would."

Jerry laughed. "Oh they'll take care of him all right. Dillon takes care of horses just about as good as he takes care of his women."

It's done and over with, Cade told himself. He took a breath.

"What's that supposed to mean?" Jenny asked.

Bart frowned. A number got called over the loud speaker. "Guess I'm in the hole. It was good seeing you, Cade." He tipped his hat and sauntered toward the chutes at the end of the show ring.

"I'm sure to be next. Don't be a stranger, you hear?" Jerry said.

"Thanks for the info." Cade took Jenny by the arm and led her in the opposite direction of the cowboys.

"Don't you worry none about that the wifey. Your secret's safe with me." Jerry winked at them.

Jenny's back stiffened.

A horn blew and the crowd whistled and applauded. A deep voice on the loud speaker announced, "Another fantastic ride! Give this cowboy another round of applause, folks."

"Did he say wife?" She froze. Her left eyebrow shot up.

"That was a long time ago." He pressed his hand into her back hoping to get her to the truck and explain on the ride home.

"So you're married?" she asked.

Frustration overwhelmed him. He raked his hand through his hair. "Not anymore."

He limped away, leaving her frowning behind him. She took off after him. "What happened?"

Crystal and Dillon had happened. He stiffened, expecting his gut to twist, but after a moment, when the sensation never came, he thanked God for easing that pain after all these years. "She left me for another cowboy."

He had enough sense not to say the rest of what he was thinking. He wondered if she would even listen to him.

"Of course she did," her voice turned chilly.

Despite whatever she believed, there was no reasoning with her here.

"Come on" he said. "There's a diner up in the next town we passed on the way here. I'll buy you a burger."

CHAPTER 36

Jenny tried not to look at the hamburger, but her stomach was so empty it growled at her. She was surprised she could think about food at all with the dismal state her life was in.

"It's got bacon and extra onions," he said.

She forced herself to smile.

"And I believe there are brownies listed under the desserts."

She loved brownies and Cade knew it. She watched him bite into his messy burger without a care in the world.

Life wasn't going the way she planned it would. She thought she had it all figured out, especially the love part. Her parents had fallen in love at first sight, and while Michael and Sarah needed a little boost they'd found their way back to each other. Obviously, she wasn't intended to live happily ever after. Brad hadn't loved her at all.

Cade … She could no longer trust him.

She wasn't going to rely on her feelings any longer. She wasn't sure she could love anyone again. Two men in so few months had broken her heart. No more of this head spinning, heart hurting rollercoaster for her.

"You need to eat something." Cade picked up a fry on the side of his plate.

"I'm fine," Jenny said. "No need to worry about me."

They were silent for a minute, then Jenny's stomach growled again.

"A few cups of coffee isn't much to go on. I'm sorry I didn't stop earlier today, but you were sleeping and I didn't want to disturb you."

"Stop." Jenny held up her hand. "Just stop."

Cade tossed down his fry. "Is this because I kissed you or because you found out I was married?"

She licked her lips nervously. "Look," she said, flattening her hand against her stomach to hold in anymore growls. "I misjudged you, Cade. I admit I misjudged a lot of things including Brad and Mr. Bailey. None of you were who I thought you were."

He had a certain glint in his eyes. She didn't want Cade to think badly of her, but he had to see how this was wrong on so many levels. After all, Brad had told her on many occasions he loved her and on the next confessed he was married.

"Not all of us are as quick to judge other people as you are."

Jenny gasped, she moved to get up and Cade grabbed her arm. "Will you sit and listen to me for once?"

Dear Lord, she prayed, please don't let me make any more mistakes that I'll come to regret later when we get home. "Sure. Whatever you have to say."

Cade let go of her and she sat back in her seat. With her shoulders pulled back, she prepared herself to listen.

"I met Crystal on the rodeo circuit. Everyone tried to talk me out of it, but I already had it in my mind to marry her. Less than a year after we married, I discovered she was two timing me with a buddy of mine, Dillon Coates. His father owns Double D ranch."

She inhaled sharply.

"She wasted no time signing the divorce papers." Cade crossed his arms, clearly on the defensive.

She sat, speechless. Silence stretching between them. Everything he said spun in her mind until she pressed her fingers to her temples.

"Can I get you anything else? Dessert? A box for that to go?" A middle aged waitress stepped up behind her.

"I think the lady will take a box to go."

Jenny pulled away from the window. She'd been watching for Cade all morning. Not constantly, of course, but here and there between doing things like filing and updating the clinic's billing. She had looked at the window half expecting to see Cade, half expecting to see the clinic's white truck.

"Something of interest outside?" Michael dropped a file folder in the basket on the corner of her desk.

"No. Not really," Jenny said, turning and walking back to her desk. "Just an empty spot where the truck and trailer are usually parked."

"I thought it might have something to do with that." Michael leaned against her desk. "Cade took off early this morning."

"You let him take the truck? What if there's an emergency call?"

"We've got Doc's truck here I can use if I needed." Michael picked up a folder on her desk and flipped through it. "I'm heading over to the clinic barn for the rest of the morning. If something comes up, you'll know where to find me. Mrs. Miller is coming over this afternoon and I figure Sarah will start to get stir crazy by lunch."

"I'll head over to check on her and the rescue as soon as Mrs. Miller gets here," Jenny said.

"Josh's got the rescue covered today."

"Knowing my brother he'll run off to who-knows-where later, and if Cade doesn't ever return someone will have to make sure the horses are taken care of."

"I believe Josh is in brake-mode. He said something about not being able to locate his truck keys."

"Maybe God has been listening to me, after all," Jenny murmured.

Michael chuckled, "Or maybe like most fathers, God knows what's best for their children and wants Josh to stay off the road today."

"Maybe." Jenny couldn't help it. She felt her lips stretch into a big grin. While she was sure it was her brother's own fault for misplacing his keys, she thought, it was about time. Now Josh couldn't run from his responsibilities.

Jenny picked up another file folder and held it out toward Michael. "I've finished inputting all the information on this one if you want to take it back over to the barn."

"I think Rascal can head back to the training with his owner early as next week," Michael tucked the folders under his arm.

"You got it," she said.

"There's left over ham and turkey subs in the fridge at the farm house for lunch," Michael said. "I appreciate you spending some time with Sarah. I know how hard this is on her to stay off her feet until the baby is born."

"Her?" Jenny asked with a laugh. "I think you mean all of us."

CHAPTER 37

Cade sat in the truck drumming his fingers on the steering wheel. Through the windshield he watched several men and women going about their everyday duties at the Double D ranch. Every once in a while someone would glance his way, and he knew he was going to have to get out or turn this truck around and go home.

He didn't drive the whole way here so he could turn back around before he found the stallion. He opened the truck door and stepped onto the ranch's soil.

Cade watched a middle aged man take long strides to reach him.

Cade shifted his weight. He reminded himself for his purpose for coming here—to get back the stallion. His ex-wife, Crystal, nor his old pal Dillon, were his concern any longer. Jenny on the other hand ... He would need to spend some more time with God sorting out his feelings about her.

"One of the boys said they thought that was you." Dale Coates greeted Cade.

Somehow the tension he expected to feel didn't bustle up inside him, though. All he could think about was Jenny's silence on the ride home from the diner last night. It was all he could do to get her off his mind on the trip here and focus on the matter at hand.

"To what do we owe the visit?" Dale crossed his arms over his plain shirted chest. A patch of gray hair sprouted from where his hair split. Other than that, Dale Coates hadn't aged much in the past few years since Cade last saw him.

"I believe you have something that belongs to me," Cade said, then he swallowed.

Dale's smile turned upside down. "I didn't take you for a man to come looking for trouble after all these years."

"I'm not looking for trouble, just my horse." Cade reached into his shirt pocket for the folded papers and held them out to Dale. "Ben Bailey's still on your payroll isn't he?"

Dale gave him a look to hold him in his place while the older man took the papers from Cade's hand. While Dale took his time reading down through them, Cade explained the situation. The older man nodded. "Bailey's a good man, does his job."

"I never knew you for one to scout rescues and shelters for stock." Cade allowed his eyes to wonder and drink in his surroundings. There were more horses in the barn or on leads than the corrals. In the past, those corrals would have been packed with horses waiting for their next rodeo gig.

"Sometimes you have to go beyond traditional methods to find what you're looking for." Dale handed back the papers. "He's not here."

"The horse or the man?" Cade asked.

Dale chuckled. "You're just like your father was, straight to the point. It's good to see you've got a good head on your shoulders these days. I heard you were out for hire these days. Word has it you're one of the best trainers when it comes to roping horses. I've got a few here in the barn ..."

"We can discuss them after *this*." Cade held up the sets of adoption papers and the letter Sarah drafted and signed for him last evening.

Dale's eyes narrowed. "You don't think much of us, here, do you?"

Cade folded the papers back up and placed them back in his shirt pocket. "I think you know where the stallion is and for reasons you're not telling me, you've got plans for that horse. If I thought any less of you than the man I know you to be, then I would have just gone to an attorney. You and I both know what a mess that can turn out to be. From what I hear, you can't afford to lose any more contracts."

Dale took a deep breath. He scratched his head in deep thought. "Why don't you come on inside the office? There's some fresh coffee and Sissy made muffins. There might be a few left on the tray," Dale nodded toward the barn. "I can at least offer you that much for coming all this way for nothing."

Outside the barn, Cade noticed their conversation had drawn curious glances from the other ranch hands. Deep creases furrowed Dale's brow and the older man's eyes softened. Cade had a feeling he hadn't come here for nothing.

There was something about the way Dale looked at him which led him to believe there was more of a reason for him coming here. "A cup of coffee sounds good."

Two men lingered outside the stables. Another hand peered at them from around the corner of a large box stall.

"You two boys make sure you bring in that second lot from the back pasture this morning before checking the fences across the way." Dale opened the door to his office inside the barn and held it open for Cade to step inside. "Help yourself."

Cade inhaled the scent of the coffee as he poured some into a black mug he found hanging near the coffee pot. Beneath his boots was a scuffed wood floor, but the mahogany desk and plush leather couch on the other side of the wall gleamed like new.

Although it didn't have the cozy welcoming feeling of Sarah's office back at Silver Wind, Cade leaned his hip against the table where he found the coffee.

"Looks like you've got yourself a nice set-up. Silver Wind Equine Rescue, uh?" Dale had seen the logo on Cade's truck door.

"It seems to me giving horses away was never your style."

"And taking things that don't belong to you is?" Cade took a hot gulp of coffee. Wincing, that hadn't come out the way he intended.

Dale hesitated. Mid reach for an empty cup near Cade, he said "You weren't the only one she hurt." He looked Cade purposefully in the eye. "She turned around and did the same thing to him, too."

Cade stared down into the black abyss of his coffee cup. He and Dillon were pals since high school. They hung out during the summers with both their fathers on the rodeo circuit. Always in competition together, even with the ladies, until they all took off to Vegas one night and Cade married Crystal. Dillon had stood beside him.

He felt a clawing at an old wound in his chest. This time the rawness of it didn't so much pain him as did the thought of it happening all over. It was within his right to feel Dillon got what he deserved, but instead Cade found himself emphasizing with this news.

Dale laid a hand on Cade's shoulder. "He found himself a pretty little filly over in Dover, and got hitched about six months ago."

Cade was speechless.

"When Bailey told me you were working at horse rescue, I thought to myself, glad to hear that boy is doing something good and moving on. Found yourself a red headed spitfire, he said."

Cade couldn't keep himself from smiling. "That's what started this mess."

"I'm afraid it isn't." Dale walked around behind his desk. "That's why I thought it best if we come in here to talk. You see, that buckskin stallion has been on my MIA list for almost two years now."

"You're saying the horse is yours?" Cade put down his cup and crossed his arms. His jaw clinched and the muscle on the side of his neck twitched.

"I know he is." Dale held up his hand. "I know how this must look to you."

"You lied."

"No. I said I don't know where he is, and I don't. I sent Bailey out to round up some new stock, and he comes and he goes as he pleases," Dale said.

"And the stallion?" Cade asked.

"He isn't here." Dale picked a photograph on his desk and held it up for Cade to see. "When you're in my kind of business, you expect to lose a few horses. I have each of them photographed. As you can see I've had many horses over the years."

Behind the desk, the office wall was a collage of horse photographs. Cade pushed away from the table, took two long strides, and snatched the photo from Dale's hand. "A lot of Buckskin horses look alike."

"This one has a brand up under his mane." Dale tapped on the photo. It was a buckskin horse with its mane clipped back far enough to show the brand on the neck. Cade searched his memory trying to capture any remembrance of Apple having a brand. There was no way he could prove for certain if the stallion did or did not. The horse's mane had long grown out and there were several scars on Apple's neck and flanks from fighting with other horses. At least, he assumed it was so. "I would have seen it if it was there."

"It matters not. A DNA test will confirm whether he is or not," Dale said.

"Since when do you record bloodlines for stock horses?" Cade couldn't deny the likeness of this photograph to Apple.

"I don't," Dale agreed. "I purchased him because his Sire is Six Degrees West."

Cade rubbed his hand over his mouth before he spoke. "That's saying the stallion is who you think he is. Six Degrees West isn't known for throwing many colts in his bloodline."

Dale grinned. "You understand now why I'd want him back."

"That's *if* he's the same horse." Cade handed back the photograph. He tucked his hand in his armpits afraid if he curled his hands into fist from his frustration he would use them to hit something.

"We'll know by tomorrow when the test comes back," Dale laid the picture back on the desk. "I wasn't lying when I said the horse wasn't here. I lost him once, I won't lose him again."

"And how was that?" Cade wondered aloud. He couldn't put his finger on it right now, but something was off about all this. He'd spent weeks with that horse and knew Apple had been at Silver Wind for almost a year. The rescue had open houses once a month allowing the public inside. "Someone stole him, am I right?"

Dale grimaced. "I made a mistake. Took a gamble and I lost."

"You have papers to prove the horse still belongs to you?" Cade could see the older man's thoughts by his facial expression. It was all Cade needed to allow relief to wash through his system. Dale Coates didn't have any legal hold on the horse any more than Ben Bailey did.

Back at Silver Wind, Apple's file would contain the surrender papers, if not a bill of sale transferring ownership of the horse to Silver Wind and then Cade.

"I have my original bill of sale. According to the ABA, the horse's papers haven't been transferred out of my name."

"Yet." Cade said, "That does not prove he is the same horse or that you have any claim on him. Now, if you'll tell me where the stallion is, I'll be taking him back to Silver Wind with me. Even if your DNA test proves a match, it doesn't change the horse's bill of sale."

"I'll tell you what." Dale walked around from behind the desk. "It'll take a few days for the vet to get the rests back from the lab. Why don't we leave Dancerman, that's the stallion's name, with our veterinarian? If the blood test comes back he's not the right horse, I'll have Bailey return the horse to you. If the stallion's DNA matches and you can bring papers proving the horse belongs to this place of yours, Silver Wind, then I'll gladly assist you in loading Dancerman onto your trailer."

Cade bit the inside his cheek, the older man had the upper hand and he knew it. "I want the name of the veterinarian and a number so Silver Wind's clinic can confirm the results."

Dale reached into his back pocket and pulled out his wallet. He slid a business card from inside the fold and handed it to Cade. "He's in good hands."

"We'll see." Cade strode out of the office. Outside, the barn yard was quit. He yanked open the door of the truck and slammed it shut. Despite his better judgment, Cade started up the truck and pulled away from the Double D with an empty trailer.

Whether the stallion was in good hands or not, he would see for himself. He taped the business card on the steering wheel and headed toward the address.

CHAPTER 38

"What?" Jenny asked as she walked over to where Sarah was sitting. She could tell by the frown that Sarah was displeased about something.

"I can't believe you did that without asking me first," Sarah said, looking tired.

Jenny sat down on the floor next to the couch where Sarah lay in the farmhouse living room. An old braided carpet covered the hardwood beneath where she sat. "I did what I thought was right. How was I supposed to know Cade adopted Apple?"

"You could have asked," Sarah said, gently.

She noticed the dark rays of orange sunlight filtering through the windows facing the front of the house. Michael and Ethan had volunteered to take care of the evening feeding chores while Jenny sat with Sarah.

Dark would come before long and there was no sign of Cade returning anytime soon.

"It's just too bad that you couldn't have allowed Cade to help you." Sarah turned to Jenny. "Michael doesn't think Cade will stay on with us now."

"Why would he think that? Cade bought the Zimmerman place. He told me." She pulled down the sleeve of her sweater and curled her fingers around the edge.

"He doesn't sign the papers until Tuesday, and when he came to me it was because he wanted to adopt Apple. I told him he needed a physical address."

"The Zimmerman place." She looked up at Sarah from picking the lint off her sleeve. "He was moving here so he could have an address to adopt Apple." She had led herself to believe he was moving into the Zimmerman place to stay closer to Silver Wind— closer to her. She'd fooled herself again.

Sarah reached down and placed her hand over Jenny's. "I think we both know there is more to it than that."

It was one thing to make a bad decision and have to admit making a mistake. It was another to end up broken hearted and then add her mistake on top of it. She'd thought long and hard about what Cade had said at the diner. "Do you know Cade was married?"

Sarah sighed and laid back deeper into the plush cushions on the couch. "Is or was?"

"Does it matter?" she asked.

"To you it does."

Jenny slid closer to the couch. She brought up her knees and wrapped her arms around her legs. She looked into the sleepy eyes of her best friend and sighed. "I don't know why I bother."

Sarah smiled. "Because you care too much, and that's why you always have to make things right, no matter what."

"Like you and Michael."

"Exactly, but sometimes when you feel something isn't right it doesn't always mean it's your place to make it so." Sarah rubbed her pregnant belly.

"And if I hadn't?"

"I would have told Michael on my own."

"But you don't know if ..."

"Neither did you. Only God knows the plans He has for us."

She didn't intend to cry. She wasn't the crying type, but her lashes grew damp and tears dripped onto her cheeks. She wiped the end of her sleeve beneath her eyes. "I'm sorry Sarah. I was afraid and I didn't want anyone else to get hurt. I knew if I waited and came to you we wouldn't agree. Silver Wind feels as if it is as much mine as it is yours."

"It is. Without you and Josh the rescue would have never happened. We're a team: you, Josh, Michael, and me. I understand why you did it, but I feel as if you sometimes take charge of things that are not yours to control. This all could have been avoided if you would have talked to me or Cade."

"Cade's our employee," Jenny dashed away more tears with her knuckles. They flowed so fast now she gritted her teeth tried to tell herself to stop crying. She wasn't a child. Only right now, she felt like one, and she didn't like this feeling of getting scolded.

"Cade is here because he voluntarily stays. We have no contract with him. He's not on the payroll, like you and Josh." Sarah said.

Jenny jumped to her feet. "I guess someone should have told us when you married Michael the partnership was only between you and him."

Sarah grabbed her hand and tried to sit up. "That's not what I meant and you know it."

"That's just it. I realize now. You have Michael and the rescue belongs to you and the clinic belongs to him and none of this is mine. Even if I wanted it too, it will never be. I'll always just be an employee, won't I?" Jenny looked at Sarah.

"You're my best friend. *Always,*" Sarah said.

Jenny lifted her chin, unable to look down at Sarah. She walked out of the living room and out the door.

Despite the warm evening air, she shivered. Stepping off the porch, she noticed the sun had turned into a darkened fiery ball hanging low in the horizon. If she kept walking straight, it appeared she would walk right into it. As she crossed the yard, Ethan shouted her name from the barn. His voice was oblivious in her thoughts.

Reaching the end of Silver Wind's lane, she looked toward home. Spying the clinic and the apartment where she lived above it caused her spirits to sink lower. This wasn't her home. This wasn't her dream. Not anymore.

Cade dropped the duffle bag at his feet. A small dog jumped and yapped at him in the clinic's waiting area.

Jenny glanced up at him, alarmed. "You're leaving?"

The circles under her eyes had darkened since the other day. Her hair was a shade darker from her usual red flare. A single clip held her bangs from covering those cat-like eyes. The sharp intensity of her stare was absent. He couldn't help wondering if this had anything to do with him.

"Returning." Cade leaned against the desk. Jenny's shoulders slumped and she glanced back at the screen on the computer. "Don't worry, I'll be out of your hair in a less than a week."

"Then that makes two of us," she said.

Cade kept looking at her. She seemed different. More than what he first thought was exhaustion. He was exhausted, driving through the night to get back here. He expected her to sass him with her words and keep him in place with those sharp eyes of hers. "If this is because I kissed you."

"It's not."

He noted the sharp tone coming back into her voice. "Then it's about the stallion?"

"No." She shook her head.

"Whatever your reasons, they'll have to wait," Cade said, pulling the veterinarian's card from his pocket. "I need your help to get him back."

"Oh." Jenny stopped. "I thought you brought him back with you."

"I have every intention of bringing him back, but now the man who has him is claiming Apple legally belongs to him."

"He can't! The contract of the adoption clearly states ..."

Cade held up his hand to silence her. "There's more to it than that. Where's Michael?"

Jenny rose and snatched the business card from Cade's hand. "He's out in the clinic checking on a pregnant mare. What's going on?"

"Any chance you can slip out to the clinic for a few minutes?" Cade asked.

"Mrs. Miller is in the back putting away supplies. She'll be taking over when I'm gone anyway." Jenny walked out from around the desk and Cade caught her by the arm. "Where do you think you're going?" he asked

"To get Mrs. Miller so I can go with you to find Michael."

He remembered what it had felt like to have her close to him, even for their brief moment when he'd kissed her up against the truck. His eyes lowered to those glossy pink lips. "That's not what I meant. You said you were leaving."

She licked her lips. Placing her hand on his chest he waited for her to shove him away, but instead she stepped closer. "I am." She admitted, "You of all people I would think would understand. I'm no longer needed here, so it's time to move on."

"I'm not going anywhere and neither are you," Cade whispered as he drew her closer to him. He cupped her face in his hands. "I need you and so does that buckskin stallion of ours."

Jenny shivered. He knew his fingers were rough and cold, but he swept his thumbs beneath her eye to catch her tears anyway. Her breath hitched, but she wasn't pulling away from him. Maybe it was because of the extra sets of eyes in the room and the silence wrapped around them. Or maybe it was because she was in shock.

Either way, he may never have this chance again. She probably expected a kiss like the last, but on the drive back from trying to rescue the stallion he decided he wasn't about to let go of Jenny, too.

He didn't need any more of an invitation then for Jenny to tilt her head in his direction. When his lips touched Jenny's he knew he'd made the right decision. His fingers were cold, but it didn't stop his lips from heating up. She trembled in his arms. He needed to stop kissing her but not as much as he needed to continue.

"There are three bottles of … Oh …" Mrs. Miller halted from down the hall with a medicine bottle in each hand.

Jenny didn't move, but Cade pulled away from her at the sound of the other woman's voice. Jenny blinked, and reached out putting her hand on the corner of the desk. "Those go on the shelf till they're opened, then they go in the refrigerator."

"Right." Mrs. Miller winked. A slow smile spread across the older woman's face.

He had forgotten they were in the clinic's waiting room. A dog whined behind Cade and its owner coughed. Jenny's face turned as red as her hair.

"I'll be back in a few minutes," Jenny said, and she fled out the clinic's front door.

Cade was relieved for the distraction and followed after her. He could tell by the way she strode out of the clinic his kiss had affected her far more deeply than she would let on.

He wouldn't let her leave Silver Wind without admitting she had feelings for him. He just prayed she could see past his previous marriage and accept him for the man who loved her.

CHAPTER 39

There was nothing more Cade could do. Michael said they would have to wait for the DNA test results. His only reassurance had come from Coates's veterinarian, ensuring the results would get faxed to Silver Wind and seeing, for himself, that Apple was safe and sound.

Had Cade not been obliged to return Michael's truck, he would found a place to stay nearby and waited. It was the waiting that made his teeth grind.

Jenny made excuses these past few days to avoid him, so he managed to busy himself with the rescue horses, filling in for Sarah, and helping Mr. Zimmerman sort and pack for his move. Cade had managed to get Mr. Zimmerman's motorcycle running. He drove it into the clinic parking lot.

During one of their evening meals Sarah shared her suspicions for Jenny's decision to leave Silver Wind. Jenny's absence at the farm house for their evening meals had started to wear on all of them. Especially, reflected in Sarah's mood. Cade could see Sarah blamed herself for what had transpired, but enough was enough.

He yanked open the clinic door. Half the lights were turned off, except for the waiting area. He found her walking out of the darkness, keys in hand. "If you need something, it will have to wait until tomorrow. We're open at eight."

Cade undid the strap beneath his motorcycle helmet and pulled it off.

Her eyes grew wide. "I didn't … You got a new motorcycle, then? Did you order from the Motorcycle shop?" She came closer edging toward the door to peer out.

"Zimmerman. He helped me get it running," Cade said, opening the door. "Take a look."

Quickly, Jenny rushed past him out the door. In the parking lot, she stood with her hands on her hips. "It's not a Harley."

Cade limped up beside her and placed his arm around her shoulders. "I guess it doesn't meet your seal of approval then?"

He felt her stiffen. "Take a ride with me. You pick the place. Let me take you out to supper."

Jenny stepped out from under his arm. "I can't."

"Can't or won't?" Cade asked, holding his helmet out toward her. "Or are you afraid?"

He saw her eyes flash with that familiar spark. That's all he needed to give him hope. She narrowed her eyes and tugged the helmet from his hands. "Just let me lock up."

He knew she wouldn't turn down his challenge. He watched her walk up to the clinic door. Helmet in one hand, keys in the other, she pulled open the door. She must have forgotten those last lights. He went to the door to wait for her.

She put down his helmet on a chair and went to her desk. A green light flashed and he walked inside. Jenny pulled the paper from the fax machine. Deeply, she frowned. Her eyes scanning the paper and then she looked at him.

"Michael will have to verify it, but I've read enough of these to know it's a match." Jenny held out the paper to him.

Cade limped across the distance and snatched the paper from her hand. He had convinced himself in all these days of waiting the odds of DNA test results coming back as a match were slim. This was one of those requests God hadn't granted him for reasons he may never understand. He took the slam in his gut as well as any man getting kicked while they were down.

She touched his arm. "I'm sorry Cade. It looks like Mr. Coates was right and Apple belongs to him."

It was never a matter of *who* was right for Cade, but *what* was right for Apple. By the look in her eyes, they were on the same mindset for once.

"Not if we have the bill of sale to prove otherwise." Cade limped over to the helmet. He held it up to her, "Ready for that ride?"

"To Sarah and Michael's place?" Jenny crossed her arms. "I don't think so."

Cade lowered the helmet in frustration. "This coming from the woman who always insists on forgiving others. Didn't you once tell me that who we are now isn't who we were in the past?"

"That's different," Jenny said.

"Because you need to see your name on a piece of paper to feel this place is as much yours as the people who own it? Coates has a piece of paper that says Apple belongs to him, but you and I both know that horse belongs here with us."

"But if Apple belongs to someone else, he should have never been brought here in the first place, so by returning him where he belongs is the right thing to do." Even though she said the words, her tone of voice said she didn't believe in what she said.

"Whether you feel Apple should have been brought here or not, the fact is he was—just like I was. I don't know about you, but given the opportunity to go back and change the past, I wouldn't stop that trailer from unhitching for anything in the world." Cade put down the helmet and drew Jenny in his arms.

She didn't resist him.

"I understand how you feel about this place. I feel it, too. Everyone here at Silver Wind … It's family. Michael and Sarah and Ethan are as much your family as Josh and your parents, and Sarah is like a sister to you. I've seen how distressed she has been over your leaving." Cade didn't like getting involved in other people's business, but he cared too much about these people to see them split apart like this.

"I don't know why. She and Michael have already replaced me with Mrs. Miller," Jenny said.

"If that were the case then why are Sarah and Michael having their lawyer draw up papers to add you and Josh to the partnership for Silver Wind?" Cade asked.

Jenny gripped his arm. "What?"

Well, that got her attention, Cade thought. "Where do you think Michael went this afternoon? He and Sarah haven't come back yet."

"They did?" I never meant … It's just that …" Jenny stopped, and then said, "They shouldn't have done that. I've made my mind up."

"And so have I." Cade dipped his head and kissed her.

Early the next morning Jenny woke to someone knocking at her door. It was a good hour until she needed to go downstairs to open the clinic. She wondered if Mrs. Miller had misunderstood her invitation to come early this morning.

When she opened the door Sarah stood holding out a pan of brownies.

"What are you doing here? Does Michael know? You're supposed to stay off your feet let alone climb these stairs!" Jenny took the pan of brownies and ushered Sarah into her small kitchen.

"Since you've not showed up for supper these past few days, I thought I would come to you." Sarah eased herself down into a chair Jenny pulled out for her.

Jenny's hands were warmed by the pan of brownies. Fresh baked and homemade and Sarah knew Jenny couldn't resist. She sat them on the table and turned to heat water to make Sarah some tea.

"I'll make something for tonight. I'm sure Michael and Josh have been bringing enough take out to last a while. "Jenny tapped her fingers on the counter anxious for the water to boil. She doubted her best friend had come here against the doctor's orders of bed rest for a friendly chat. She couldn't bring herself to turn toward Sarah until she heard, "You know Josh; he's not around much."

"But he's been helping at the rescue and cleaning the stalls at the clinic. Sarah shook her head. "Cade's been taking care of it, which hasn't left him much time to work with the horses."

Thoughtfully, Jenny pulled a mug from the peg near her coffee pot. She placed a tea bag inside as the kettle whistled. "I'll speak to him."

"But it's not your place." Sarah shifted in her seat.

Jenny flinched She took a deep breath, about to speak when Sarah said, "You know it's a shame you're leaving so soon. I had hoped you would be here for when the baby was born. I don't know if I can do this without you."

Jenny laughed and tried to wave Sarah's comment off. "You don't need me. You have Michael. This is his chance to be there for you now when he couldn't be there for you before."

While inside she was thought, Lord, why are you doing this to me?

"Without Gram, and now you ..."

Steam warmed her cheeks as she poured the hot water into the mugs. She tried to draw her emotions back in check.

"It's not my place anymore." Jenny meant what she said, but she didn't feel it. Sarah was going to need her help more than ever. She was right. Sarah's grandmother was gone, and all she had left was Michael and Ethan for family. But that wasn't true. Michael's family was Sarah's family now, too. His father stopped in from time to time and Michael took Sarah and Ethan to visit for important dates, but they weren't here—not like she was. Josh wasn't even here when she needed him anymore.

"I can't help feeling I've done something, but I don't know what it is or how to fix it. Tell me what it is you want that will make you stay? I've gone to our lawyer and the paperwork is all in order. The Silver Wind Equine Rescue is as much yours and Josh's as it is mine, but it's still a non-profit. There is no land or assets beyond what's in the rescue barn." Sarah scooted her chair back to leave.

"It's not you. Please don't go." Jenny looked back over her shoulder. When Sarah relaxed in her seat, Jenny said, "After all, you did break doctor's orders to bring me these brownies. It doesn't seem right not to have them, and the tea's ready."

"I had Michael take me to Louisville yesterday. He didn't like it, but I didn't give him much of a choice," Sarah pulled the sugar bowl on the table closer as Jenny set down a hot steaming mug of tea in front of her.

"Cade told me." Jenny retrieved the brownies. She glanced at the clock to check the time, out of morning habit.

"I hoped he would." Sarah took a spoon Jenny offered her. "I know what it feels like to want something of your own, and I understand there are certain voids in our lives we can't fill for each other. If you would stay and give it some time, then I think you'd find what you're looking for is still here."

"I'm sorry." Jenny sat down across from Sarah at the table. "I appreciate what you're trying to do, but it's more than that and I think you know it."

"Trust in the Lord and seek Him in all things first. Sound familiar?" Sarah put a spoonful of sugar in her tea and stirred.

"Yes." Jenny tried not to smile.

"Still leaving?" Sarah asked.

"Once I finish training Mrs. Miller and help Cade settle this business about Apple," Jenny said.

"Then I pray it doesn't ever get settled." Sarah put down her spoon.

"Sarah. Why would you say that? Cade loves that horse," Jenny said, muttering, "I don't know why after all the trouble that stallion has caused."

"I can think of someone else he loves and could say the same thing about, too."

Jenny didn't try to stop the smile she knew had formed on her face. She'd climbed aboard his vintage motorcycle and held tight onto him as he took her out for dinner. She felt her face flush, and this time it wasn't from the steam of hot water splashing out of the kettle.

"Where did Josh say he got Apple from? I checked the file and there are no surrender papers from the previous owner." Jenny asked, trying to change the subject.

"I don't know." Sarah frowned.

"What do you mean you don't know?"

"Well, I don't know. I don't think Josh ever said where he got him from."

Jenny jumped to her feet. "If we can't prove Apple belongs to the rescue then we may not get him back, and if we don't get him back ..."

Sarah grinned, "Prayer answered. You have to stay."

Jenny's scowl made Sarah laugh, but as far as Jenny was concerned this was no laughing matter. She had to find Josh.

CHAPTER 40

There was a plaid shirt lying on the arm of the couch. Cade spied the dark splotch of dried blood on the sleeve and scooped it up. A few feet from the couch a cowboy boot lay on the floor and near the bathroom another.

Sometime in the early hours of morning his roommate had returned. This wasn't new, but the stained shirt was. He suspected Josh would sleep most of the day, but this didn't sit well with his gut. Cade strode down the hall to the other man's room and knocked on the door.

No answer.

He knocked again louder and heard a groan from the other side of the door. He tried to open the door, but something was blocking it. He pushed harder, shoving the door and shoving the blockage aside. Except what blocked it was Josh's body sprawled out on the floor.

Josh lay a few feet from his bed with his t-shirt pulled up over his head and his arms trapped inside it. Several bruises spotted Josh's sides. Cade eased himself down on his good leg and checked to make sure Josh still breathed. He was fortunate he hadn't suffocated himself with his t-shirt, but that didn't bring Josh any sympathy from Cade.

He yanked down Josh's shirt. Josh howled with pain and jerked back.

"Good to see you're awake. Rough night?" Cade asked.

Josh curled himself away from Cade and covered his face with his hands. Cade heard muffled attempts to tell him to get out and mind his own business, but they also fell short as Josh's eyes watered.

"It wouldn't surprise me if that jaw of yours was broken along with your nose." Cade pushed himself up off the floor. Standing he held out his hand to Josh. "We'd best get you some medical attention before your face goes from looking like a grape to a blueberry. I'll go grab some ice and call Jenny."

Josh grabbed Cade's arm. He shook his head and croaked, "No Jen-ny."

Cade helped Josh to his feet. He made him sit down on the bed before he fell down. "Fine. Where's your truck keys?"

Josh reached in his jean pocket.

"You sure you don't want me to call your sister?"

By the look in Josh's eyes, Cade could see he didn't. He put his arm around Josh and helped him out of the carriage house. Josh's truck was parked by the side of the house with no trailer hitched. He got Josh into the passenger side, did a quick glance around for the missing trailer, then climbed behind the wheel of the Josh's truck.

Later, he would ask Josh what kind of trouble he was in. He had a feeling Josh was in something deeper than he realized. He prayed for Jenny's sake it wasn't too late to turn the situation around.

With Sarah back at the farm house and Mrs. Miller overseeing the clinic appointments, Jenny headed to the rescue barn. Expecting to find Josh, she was disappointed to see Cade working with a sorrel mare out in the corral.

"Have you seen Josh?" She'd spied her brother's truck by the barn and her need to speak with him rose at an alarming rate.

Cade slowed the mare's trot on the lunge line and looked at her. "I sent him home."

"Why?" Jenny marched over to Cade. "The stalls haven't been cleaned!"

"I'll take care of it when I get done here. It's not like I haven't done it before," Cade smooched to the horse as Jenny walked up beside him.

"You could stick around and give me hand if you'd like." His gaze on her sent tingles like little electric shocks zinging through her. She took a step away from him deciding it best to distance herself from him. There was no way, she told herself, she was going to get attached to him and have him break her heart like Brad had.

"I still need to speak with my brother. Knowing him, he'll be running off somewhere before I can catch him again," Jenny said.

"I'd wait until later. He had a rough night last night," Cade turned with the horse running now in a circle.

Jenny turned with him. "He's going to have it a whole lot rougher if he doesn't tell me where he got that stallion from."

"Whoa now, Whoa," Cade said, and even though he spoke to Jenny the mare on the other end of the line came to a halt.

"You haven't' changed your mind about getting the stallion back have you?" Jenny crossed her arms and shifted her stance.

"No."

"Then I'm going to talk to my brother." Jenny turned on her heal and Cade caught her by the arm. He drew her close. "We'll both go talk to Josh after supper tonight. I could really use your help here at the barn."

Jenny's arms itched to wrap around him and her heart begged for the right to do so. He must have read her mind as a new set of tingles exploded inside her when he pulled her into his arms. She closed her eyes as he lowered his lips to hers. His hand came up around the base of her neck and she wrapped her arms around his neck needing to get closer to him. Tenderness and emotion mixed and swirled in her heart.

"There is someplace I'd like to take you this Tuesday," he said after pulling away from her. "Can you manage to get away from the clinic for an hour or two around lunch?"

"Wh-where are we going?"

Behind them the mare tugged on the line and Cade pulled on it drawing the horse to him. "I can't tell you, or it wouldn't be a surprise."

She felt heartsick. She'd had enough sour surprises these past few months. She didn't want anymore, but like a kid on Christmas morning, curiosity would get the best of her.

The afternoon had slipped away and with it, so had Jenny. While she retreated to the farm house to prepare supper, he finished cleaning up and promised to bring Josh with him for their evening meal.

"Feeling better?" Cade found Josh in the kitchen with a bowl of soup heating in the microwave.

Josh had a wide piece of tape across his face and bruising on one side of his face. "What do you think?"

"I think someone busted your nose right good and you're lucky they didn't break your jaw," Cade said.

Josh looked at him through swollen eyes. "Trailer door slammed into my face," Josh muttered.

Cade shook his head. "Slammed into your ribs, too, uh?"

Josh tried to scowl, but it came out more of a wince. Behind him the microwave beeped. "Forget it. Not your problem."

"Didn't see your trailer parked anywhere, lose it?" Cade had a sinking feeling along with his suspicions. He knew he was pushing when he asked, "How much do you owe this time?"

Josh was silent for a long time. He took the bowl of soup and sat down at the table. He stirred the noodles in the broth and stared at the spoon. Cade leaned against the counter and crossed his arms feeling more like an older brother than a friend. "If you'd rather have this conversation with Jenny ..."

Josh looked up, "You didn't tell her."

"Not unless you tell me," Cade said. "She's expecting you up at the farm house for supper."

"I can't," Josh said.

"Whatever kind of trouble you're in ..."

"I can take care of it." Josh huffed. With his nose stuffed and patched, he was forced to breath with his mouth.

"Your family will understand. I'm sure they'll help you," Cade said.

Josh put his head in his hands and shook his head. "I don't need anyone telling me how to run my life. You've been around my sister enough, you should know."

Cade did know. He also knew Josh couldn't handle this alone. Too many times he saw men fall to their lowest, desperate to rise, and unable to stop themselves from doing the same things over and over again that pulled them down in the first place.

"Fine, but I need your help."

Slowly, Josh looked up. "What's in it for me?"

"How about two Tylenols, an excuse for supper and a way to get your trailer back?" Cade asked.

"I'm listening," Josh said.

"Tell me where you got the stallion from and give me the papers I need to prove he belongs to the rescue, so I can adopt him. Then I'll pay off your debt to get your trailer back and you can work off your debt by giving me a hand over at the old Zimmerman place."

"And you won't tell Jenny?"

"That's between you and you're sister," Cade said.

Josh took his outstretched hand and they shook on it. "We'll take care of the paper work in the morning."

Taking care of Jenny was a different matter. He wouldn't lie to her, but he hoped he could distract her long enough for Josh to overcome this and tell her on his own. It was the one thing he felt would keep her from leaving Silver Wind—and him.

CHAPTER 41

Tuesday morning arrived with the promise of cooler temperatures. Muck boots on and barn coat zipped Jenny trudged to the rescue barn. She hadn't seen much of Cade nor her brother these past few days. On Sunday Cade had sat beside her in church, taking her hand in his as they listened to the message. Josh had showed up for dinner with her parents, but it hadn't escaped her attention that Cade and her father had been deep in conversation while her mother fussed over Josh.

She laughed when her mother suggested Josh go get an eye exam after getting slammed in the face by a trailer gate. It wasn't funny, she knew, but it didn't cause her any less concern for him. As his twin, she felt there was something wrong. Something Josh wasn't telling them.

Normally, she'd demand he tell her, but seeing his injuries, his prolonged trips away from Silver Wind, she prayed instead for Josh to find his way. No one else could understand this feeling, she realized, of being lost.

A thick frost coated the grass and left tracks of her foot prints across the distance from her car to the barn. Inside the sounds of horses awakening greeted her. She slid the barn door open enough to squeeze through and spotted Josh coming around the corner with a bale of hay.

It made her smile.

Or maybe it was the smell of fresh hay.

Or maybe, just maybe, it was because today was the day Cade had a surprise for her. It was a good surprise, or she told herself it was. She was looking forward to spending time with him after not seeing him since Sunday.

If she didn't know better she would think Josh and Cade were keeping something from her.

"Aren't you supposed to be over at the clinic or something?" Josh dropped the bale of hay and pulled out his pocket knife to cut the twine.

"Today is Michael's day for farm visits and Doc isn't in till this afternoon, so I thought I'd come help with the horses this morning. Is Cade around?"

Josh flipped his pocket knife closed and stuffed it in his back pocket. Other than the bruising still around his eye and cheek bone, his nose didn't appear to have been broken. "No, he had business to attend to and said he'd be back later."

Jenny heard something bang down on one of the stall doors and noticed movement in Apple's old stall. She hurried past Josh.

"Apple!" The stallion backed into the corner of his stall. His head up, eyes wide, and his nostrils flaring, as if she were some great enemy come to do him harm. His front feet were splayed, and his thick black mane hung past his neck, nearly to his chest. His coat was wheat gold.

She'd never seen him so clean. Jenny whirled around. "When did he come back?"

"I picked him up yesterday and brought him back," Josh said.

"Does Cade know?"

Apple blew hard through his nostrils.

Josh reached in his pocket and offered a few pieces of carrots he had stashed. "He's the one who sent me to fetch him."

"So he does belong to the rescue? All the paperwork is in order?" Jenny took the carrots from him.

"He belonged to me and I surrendered him to the rescue," Josh said.

"Where did you get him?" Her heart tightened and she held out a carrot for Apple.

"Let's just say I found him in a bad way and his owner owed me money." Josh divided the hay in chunks and started stuffing hay racks in the stalls beside Apple's.

"And the papers?" She needed to know.

"In a shoebox," Josh said as if she should know that.

"And they just gave him back?" Jenny asked.

"I'm sure we haven't heard the last from them, but Cade didn't leave them much of a choice." Josh swiped away the hay clinging to his jacket. "Whatever Cade had that lawyer write in that letter I handed to your Mr. Coates made his boss stammering mad."

"I'm just glad you and Apple are back here safe." Jenny turned back to Apple who hadn't taken her offer of carrot pieces.

"You still plan on leaving here?" Josh asked.

Jenny shrugged. " Maybe."

"You know, you'll be more miserable living with mom and dad then you are here," Josh said.

"That's what Sarah tells me."

"Maybe you should listen to her for a change," Josh said, before walking away.

"I wish I had an apple. Then you would be my friend wouldn't you? Or at least long enough to get the apple," Jenny said to the horse.

Apple backed up even further, smashing himself into the corner. She continued to talk quietly to him, holding out the carrot.

The buckskin stallion trembled, and sweat seeped into the matted hair of his chest.

Could it be that Apple was terrified of her?

His head wove back and forth, his eyes so wide she could see the white rims. Maybe she'd been wrong about him all this time. Her hand grew tired of holding the carrot and she let it drop to her side. "I don't blame you. I wouldn't want a carrot either if I could have an apple, instead."

She tossed the carrot in his feeder. "Just in case you change your mind."

At the sound of the carrot hitting the empty feeder, Apple flinched.

Jenny clenched her fists against the urge to reach out and sooth the frightened stallion. All she wanted was to hug him, hold him, to make him realize that everything was going to be okay now. He was home now. He was safe. But she knew to reach out to him now would make him go berserk in his stall.

Cade, she was certain, could sooth him. Horse and man had a bond, one she understood. As she, too, had grown attached to the man as well.

She stood there for another minute, watching the buckskin stallion flatten against the far wall of his stall. It hadn't been so long ago he'd tried to trample them, run them down, and gain his freedom. He turned his head away from her, his body trembling and his neck soaked with sweat.

How could she have ever let this happen?

If only she had known this would happen. She'd ignored Cade's warnings. No, not ignored. She'd refused to acknowledge them.

The stallion shuddered and quickly she started talking. "I named you, you know. Called you Apple and everyone laughed, but what they didn't know is that I really called you Apple Blossom. I suppose that would seem even sillier to call a stallion Apple Blossom. But do you know why?

Because I love apple blossoms. I love everything about them. They're so pure and beautiful, and from within them comes something miraculous. I love their smell, the taste of their fruit, and I love watching the wind carry a petal in the breeze on a warm spring day. Most of all, you know what I love …"

She grabbed the bars of his stall door. Closing her eyes, she leaned her forehead against the cold black metal. Sarah was never going to let her live this one down. How could she have been so foolish?

Her eyes flew open at the sound of a carrot bitten in two.

It was a little after one in the afternoon when Cade pulled up to the clinic and found Jenny pacing the parking lot. He knew he was late, but the paperwork at the realtor's office had taken far longer than expected.

He pulled up alongside her. She didn't appear mad nor happy as she took the helmet she had been holding in one hand and slipped it on. He held out his hand and helped her climb behind him. Revving the engine with his thumb, he waited for the tremble in his hands to still. Feeling her press against his back and give both his sides a squeeze, the signal he taught her, that she was ready to go, he drove them out of the parking lot and toward the old Zimmerman place.

He relaxed, enjoying having her riding along with him. When the farm lane came into view, he almost missed the turn. He knew she recognized where he was taking her, he hoped she wouldn't guess his purpose.

By now, she would know of the stallion's return. So far, Josh was keeping his part of their agreement. It had cost him far more than he expected to pay on Josh's debt to have the trailer returned. A decision he prayed he would not come to regret later.

Mr. Zimmerman had left the old truck parked in front of the house. Another gift, along with some furnishings inside the house to help Cade get settled. Pulling up by the old truck, Cade cut the engine off and looked back at Jenny through his face mask. He pulled up the shield and said, "I hope you're still hungry. I ordered lunch for us at the Café in town and set it up for us in the kitchen."

She gripped his shoulders while she swung her leg out and climbed off the back of his motorcycle. "That's where you went this morning. This is your place now, isn't it?"

Cade unbuckled his helmet and pulled it off. He waited for her to do the same and set the helmets on the motorbike seat. "Want to come inside?"

"That's why we're here isn't it?" Jenny said.

He couldn't tell by the tone of her voice if she sounded annoyed or disappointed with him. He'd taken her hand and led her up on the porch. It wasn't as large as Silver Wind, but he hoped it would warm her heart as it did him.

He reached in his pocket for the keys and hesitated. He thought about this moment a lot these past few days.

"Don't tell me you planned on a picnic here on the porch. I know its October, but it's still a little chilly to stay outside." Jenny put her free hand in her pocket.

"Actually I was thinking I'd carry you through the door way," Cade said.

"Why would you want to do that," she asked, alarmed, looking up at him with those big green eyes of hers.

"Because I'd like this place to be as much your home as it is mine." Cade took a deep breath and took both of Jenny's hands in his.

"*Really?*" Jenny said. "If you think because you were married once that I'd just move in with you then you don't know me."

Cade laughed softly, "Oh I know you alright, Jenny Anderson. I know you to be the most head strong woman I've ever met, but a woman with one of the biggest hearts I've ever seen. A woman who'd do anything to protect those she loves and stand up for what she believes is right. A woman who is filled with true faith and grit that I've come to love."

Her eyes bore into his. Looking into those big, beautiful eyes, Cade lost all thought of the farm around them.

"You really think so," she said softly, raising their joined hands between them and stepping closer.

"Really," Cade said.

She grinned and her eyes filled with tears. "I love you, too."

"It's a might hard for me to get down on one knee," Cade said.

Jenny shook her head. "Then don't."

"I wanted to make sure this was done right. I know how important that is to you, so I asked your father. With his permission given, will you marry me?"

Jenny went still. He watched her eyes widen with disbelief. "I thought you wanted this place because of Apple. You were so insistent on having him back."

He felt his heart would explode. How he loved this woman! "Only because I didn't want you to be without your confidant, I know how much you confide in that horse and how special he is to you."

A slow smile spread across her face. "Perhaps one day, you'll teach our children to ride on him. I would like to have a bunch— kids, not horses. But horses, too ..."

He silenced her with a kiss. "I'll take that as a yes," he said, before kissing her again.

"Indeed," Jenny smiled against his lips.

Cade leaned back. "Well now that it is settled." He unlocked the door to the house and pushed open the door.

Jenny squealed and laughed as he swept her up in his arms.

"We've got a threshold to cross," he used his lame leg to hold the screen door open.

"Whoa there!" She said, "What exactly do you think you're doing?"

"Taking you inside," Cade said. "Unless you'd rather have that picnic here on the porch."

"In that case, carry on." Jenny sighed and sent up a silent thank you as she rested her head on his shoulder. This was her place in more ways than one, and she had no intentions of ever leaving this place again.

EPILOGUE

On a Sunday afternoon, with the first flakes of snow drifting in the November air Jenny stood in a Sunday School room and gazed at her reflection in the mirror. Her mother's gown had been lovingly repurposed for this occasion.

"You are such a beautiful bride," Sarah slipped a bobby pin up under Jenny's veil to hold it in place.

Jenny leaned toward Sarah, her best friends' protruding belly obstructing her reach. She was a sight to hold in her empire waist burgundy gown and cowboy boots.

Jenny's cowboy boots peeked from beneath her gown's hem. It had taken every excuse they could come up with for Josh to lure their mother away from Jenny so she could slip them on instead of the silhouettes her mother insisted she wore.

"You ready?" Josh poked his head around the doorway. "They're lighting the candles now and Dad's waiting by the Sanctuary entrance. No telling how long before Mom will try to slip back here and cry all over you if you don't show up soon."

Brother and sister exchanged knowing glances. Jenny lifted the end of her gown. "More than I'll ever be." Jenny couldn't believe she was getting married.

Sarah gave her a quick hug. "I'll go out first. I won't want to block anyone's way." She smiled and picked up a cluster of mums with glittered leaves tied together.

"Oh, my veil." Jenny tried to reach behind her.

"I got it." Josh reached around her and brought the thin layer up over her head.

"Thank you," she whispered as they walked out of the room.

"Better you than me." Josh peered around the corner and motioned for her to follow him.

"You're next." Her next breath was taken away by the flickering candles in the sanctuary along with the fall foliage and warm tones of ribbons on the pews. Catching sight of Cade standing inside waiting for her, she froze.

Josh gently nudged her forward, "Not if you don't keep marching up that aisle."

She couldn't take her eyes off him. Michael and Ethan stood by his side. Along with their family and friends, the good people of Shelbyville filled the pews.

"Coming Jenny?" her father held out his arm to her.

Sarah had started her descant down the aisle and Jenny saw her mother back up and take her seat in front. Her poor mother had been so distressed when she and Cade announced they would wed in a month. Neither one of them wanted to waste any time on starting their future.

"You don't want to keep him waiting," Josh put his hand on the small of her back and guided her to their father.

"Oh I'm not." Jenny hugged her brother. "Sarah's given me plenty of time."

"Time for what?" Josh asked.

"To remember this moment."

Josh scoffed.

"Someday a girl will come along and capture your heart. You'll see. Then you'll stop running and you'll appreciate this moment, as I am." Jenny gave her brother one last squeeze before taking her father's offered arm.

Josh walked up the aisle and sat beside his mother as the

organ music filled the sanctuary.

It was time. She took a deep breath and stepped forward. She had eyes only for Cade. Even as her father placed her hand in Cade's, her eyes never left his. Her hands trembled as they said their vows and exchanged rings. In a blink, Cade was lifting her veil.

"You may kiss the bride."

Cade did and she felt his love clear down to her toes.

ACKNOWLEDGEMENTS

Writing a book is a team effort, and I couldn't have done this without the support of the West Branch Christian Writers and Saint Davids Christian Writers.

A special thanks to my editor, Norma Matson, my husband, Chad, who formats and typesets all my books, and Grace who is always keeping me motivated to write.

I'm grateful for my beta readers whose feedback has proven invaluable to me.

Thanks to my Facebook friends at 'Susan Lower, Author' and Twitter friends for all the encouragement and enthusiasm for this project.

To my family: Chad, Isabella, Malachi, and Alessandra. I love each one of you so much! Thank you for the cups of tea, helping around the house, and believing in me.

Lastly, thank you, friend, for letting me share this story with you. I couldn't do this if it wasn't for you. I enjoy connecting with readers like you through my Facebook group and on Twitter. Visit my website at www.SusanLower.com. I'd love to hear from you.

ABOUT THE AUTHOR

The daughter of a dairy farmer, Susan grew up watching westerns and riding horses. While at college, she met and married a man allergic to her beloved horses. Now the only horses she stables are the ones in her books.

Susan and her family reside in Pennsylvania near the home of the Little League World Series. When she's not writing about horses, heroes, or hope, Susan enjoys reading, book binding, watching movies, traveling, and doing crafts and sewing projects. To learn more about Susan's books, visit her at: http://www.susanlower.com.

Made in the USA
Charleston, SC
22 May 2016